A Bid on Forever

JOY AVERY

A BID ON FOREVER

First Print Edition: March 2019

ISBN-13: 978-1-797-41541-3

DEDICATION

Dedicated to the dream.

DEAR READER,

As always, THANK YOU for your support of **#joyaveryromance**. I am overwhelmed by your dedication and support. I'm also highly grateful. You will never know how much I appreciate you, but I'll try to show you by continuing to bring you beautiful love stories.

I had so much fun penning Macie and Trent's love journey. I hope you enjoy reading it as much as I enjoyed writing it. If you believe in second chances, you'll root for these two every step of the way. They deserve their happily ever after.

Please help me spread the word about A BID ON FOREVER by recommending it to friends and family, book clubs, social media and online forums. I'd also like to ask that you take a moment to leave a review on the site where you purchased this book. Reviews help to keep our love stories alive!

I love hearing from readers. Feel free to email me: authorjoyavery@gmail.com

Until next time, be blessed and happy reading!

P.S.: Be sure to check out the others books in the Distinguished Gentlemen series. You'll find a title list at the back of this book.

ACKNOWLEDGMENTS

My thanks—first and foremost—to God for blessing me with this gift of storytelling.

My endless gratitude to my husband and daughter for your unwavering support and patience. I love you both very much!

To my friends and family who've offered tons and tons of encouragement and support, I express my greatest gratitude. Your support means the world to me.

To my readers. I'm grateful for each and every one of you.

Last, but definitely not least… To my Joyrider Street Team, you ladies are the absolute best. Thank you for choosing to ride with me. I look forward to enjoying many more miles with y'all!

One

Only one person could have gotten Trent Thatcher back to Southlake Park. Especially in frigid March. But when Mama Peaches—a.k.a, Mama of Chicago—had called to say she needed him, he hadn't hesitated for one second returning to the place that had brought him so much joy—and respectively had caused him so much pain.

Anything for Mama Peaches, the woman who helped to sculpt him into the man he was today, including agreeing to be one of several bachelors up for auction at the charity event happening in three days. He fought a groan.

How bad could it be?

The tiny voice that lurked in everyone's head, just waiting to wreak havoc, took the opportunity to remind him he'd be spending hours entertaining a complete stranger. That changed his perspective.

It could be bad. Really bad.

Brushing the thoughts of doom away, Trent performed a full circle in the spacious living room inside the old Victorian. A few things had changed. The cherry-colored sectional, mahogany end and cocktail tables, and brass floor lamps had all been replaced with a slate gray sofa, loveseat, and chaise lounger, pewter tables, and intricate overhead lighting. Thick moss green and gold curtains were now an earthy brown and sheer, allowing an abundance of light to penetrate the room. While he liked the update, the modern flair kind of surprised him.

Scrutinizing more of the house where he'd spent countless hours escaping his own reality, his gaze landed on the numerous frames lining the mantle above the crackling stone fireplace. Nearing it, he delicately removed one. Staring down at the image captured in the shot unleashed a beast of memories. Some good. Some not so good.

With a gentle touch, he traced a finger over the glass protecting the photo underneath. Macie Shaw. The ultimate love of his life. *Until things went so wrong.* Sadness clenched his chest. This woman should have been his wife. Should have been his forever.

"She's a gorgeous thing, isn't she?"

The sound of Mama Peaches' voice behind him, jolted him from his trance. *Yes, she is.* However, he didn't allow the words to move beyond a fading thought in his head. He eyed Mama Peaches. With her flawless brown skin, at seventy-four, Mama Peaches could have easily passed for a woman in her fifties, possibly even forties, if it wasn't for the headful of silky gray hair she sported.

Mama Peaches laughed. "You two were something else. Reminded me so much of me and my Harold. God rest his soul."

Her dark brown eyes sparkled, and she paused for a moment, a smile touching her lips as if reliving a beautiful memory. Trent didn't interrupt the recaptured moment. Several seconds later, Mama Peaches snapped out of it.

"Lord, we can spend a lifetime living in the past, ignoring the gift of the present God's given us."

Didn't he know it.

She studied the picture he still held. "That was taken about a month back. At the annual sock drive. It was cold as unrepented sin out there, but so worth our efforts. And thank you again for the several boxes of socks you sent. There are a lot of men, women, and children walking around with warm feet because of you."

"I was happy to help," Trent said.

A month ago. Obviously, Macie had come back home for a visit. Shamelessly, something he hadn't done since he'd moved away three years ago. Visiting had been too hard for a number of reasons, but he'd kept in touch. Which was how he'd known Macie had gotten engaged and moved away a year or so ago. A cop, if he remembered correctly.

For whatever foolish reason, the thought of Macie being another man's wife felt like rusty, jagged nails being dragged slowly across his skin. At one point, she had been his only reason for living.

Scattering the demons of his past, he replaced the wooden enclosure and joined Mama Peaches by the sofa. Always the gracious host, she'd prepared food, despite his protest. Truthfully, he was glad she hadn't listened to him because he was starving. After landing and retrieving his rental car, he'd driven straight here instead of the hotel.

Excusing himself to wash up, he rejoined Mama Peaches in the living room. She patted the space beside her and flashed one of those warm and welcoming smiles she was known throughout the Southlake Park neighborhood for. And just as it had numerous times before, it soothed him.

"Sit down. I made your favorite."

Trent's stomach growled at the mere notion of biting into one of the crustless chicken salad sandwiches layered perfectly on the silver tray, alongside fresh-cut veggies, a mound of chips and a glass of her famous iced tea. Though living in the south for the past three years, he wasn't sure how his palette would respond to unsweetened tea now. He'd gotten used to drinking it syrupy sweet. North Carolina had spoiled his taste buds.

Once Mama Peaches had blessed the food, he dug in, finishing his first sandwich in less than three bites and snatching up a second. He'd forgotten how good her homemade chicken salad was. And even better than he remembered.

"Lord, look at you go. Still got that ferocious appetite. Eat all you want. There's plenty more where that came from."

He believed her. Food had never been a shortage inside this house. When tears filled her eyes, Trent stopped mid chew, a knot tightening in his stomach. "What's wrong?"

"Nothing." She patted him on the leg. "Just so happy my gent is here." She rested a hand on his cheek. "I missed you, my boy."

Gent. Trent hadn't heard the term in so long he'd nearly forgotten about the endearment Mama Peaches used for the young men she fostered—or "unofficially" fostered, in his case. He swallowed and placed the remainder of the sandwich down. "I'm sorry I haven't visited. I've been…" His word dried up shy of offering her a plethora of excuses. The woman who'd made sure he had clean clothes to wear, food in his stomach and provided all the things his mother couldn't deserved more than empty explanations.

"Don't you apologize. You've been living your life, which is exactly what you should be doing. You're here now," she said. "You're here when I need you. And that's all that matters. Like I always say, life isn't only about where you're going, it's about not forgetting where you came from. You haven't forgotten. Evident by your being here now, showing your support."

Sometimes it felt like he had forgotten. And sometimes it was on purpose. He nodded but still felt a ping of regret for staying away for so long. His gaze drifted across the room, landing on the picture frame he'd held earlier.

"I still wish you would stay here," she said, "instead of some cold, damp hotel room."

He fixed his mouth to address her comment, but what slipped out was, "How is she?"

"Why don't you ask her yourself?"

Trent eyed Mama Peaches and chuckled. "I'm not sure her husband would appreciate me reaching out to his wife." The use of the term *his wife* nagged him.

"She's okay," Mama Peaches said.

The way Mama Peaches said it—cautiously, uncertain—caused a small hint of concern to rise up inside him. What was she leaving unsaid? And was Macie truly okay?

***

Macie Shaw wasn't sure why she was even entertaining her best friend's suggestion of online dating and even more dumbfounded as to why she'd allowed Collette to create a profile on the Cozy Connections site for her. Yes, Macie agreed that it was time to *get back out there,* but what happened to meeting someone the old-fashioned way: bumping into each other at the grocery store, a hook-up by friends, a close encounter on the basketball court.

At the latter, she smiled a bit. The thought took her back to a time years in the past to a man she'd believed would be her future, her forever. Sadness washed over her. Neither heartbreak, a broken engagement, nor time had faded her memories of Trent Thatcher. But how could it? At one point they'd been so close it felt as if they shared one soul.

For fun—or possibly necessity—she imagined Trent a hundred pounds heavier and prematurely balding. The visual made her laugh, and so did the ridiculous notion, because Trent had always been in perfect shape with a body that could turn the head of a nun.

"Yeah, he does look a bit homely, doesn't he? And he's

definitely not thirty-six. Maybe forty-six. Why do men lie about their age? That's a woman's territory. They should stay out of it."

Shaking the thoughts of her ex away, Macie shifted her head from one side to the other. "I don't know. He's not *that* bad."

"Okay, that's just desperation talking. You're longing for a donging. Trippin' for a dickin'. We really need to get you laid."

Macie parted her lips to dispute Collette's claim, but realized her friend might just have a point. What had it been, six months? Yep, Collette had been spot-on. She needed to get laid. The bed-shaking, back-breaking kind of lay that Tr— She caught herself. Lately, her thoughts of Trent refused to stay where they belonged. *In the past.*

"Okay, this one has potential. Look at those dimples," Collette said.

Macie studied the screen. "Not bad."

"I'm glad you think so. Click."

Macie's eyes widened. "*Click*? What do you mean click? You didn't just..."

Collette flashed a wicked grin. "I did. You can thank me later."

"Thank you?" Macie lifted her hands. "I'm about to strangle you."

"You need this, Mace. You spend all of your free time here." Collette fanned her hands around the dry cleaners Macie owned. "It took me threatening bodily injury for you to take a vacation next week. Even if this leads nowhere, at least you get to enjoy a great night with a handsome man."

"How do you know it'll be great? He could turn out to be a fraud. Or worse, a psycho."

"You read too many thriller novels. I met Jeremy online, remember? And look at us."

Collette did have a point there, too. She'd met the man of her dreams online. They were approaching a year together. Macie had to admit, she'd never seen her friend happier. Still, that didn't mean this would work out so well for her. Macie groaned to herself. At thirty-four, shouldn't she have had her life together? A husband, kids. The only worthwhile thing she'd accomplished was owning her own business. These days, it was the only thing that brought her joy.

"You're never going to meet someone new if you never go out. It's not like your soulmate is going to saunter through that door and sweep you off—"

The chime drew both their attentions to the front of the store. A second later, they burst into laughter over the ironic timing.

"I'll be right with you," Macie called out, then turned to Collette. With a smirk, she said, "You were saying? This could be my soulmate now, coming to lay claim to me." Laughing, she headed to the front.

"Welcome to—" When the visitor turned, Macie stopped dead in her tracks, her heart leaping into her throat. Was she hallucinating? Was he really here, or was her overactive imagination playing tricks on her? She blinked several times. Nope, he was still there. And the quiver in her stomach told her this was no illusion. She swallowed hard. "*Tr-Trent?*"

The blank expression on his face suggested he was just as stunned to see her as she was to see him. As suspected, he'd kept himself in tiptop shape and was far finer than she remembered. Was he taller? Did thirty-six-year-old men experience growth spurts? No, she convinced herself. He was more than likely still the six-two he'd been when he'd left Chicago. Without her.

Collette came from the back, probably expecting a glimpse of a possible soulmate for her friend. The scream that came from Collette jarred Macie from her stupor.

"Trent Thatcher!" Collette hurried across the room, practically throwing herself into Trent's arms. While he wrapped his arms around the excited woman, his eyes never left Macie.

Collette had always liked Trent and had been the lone voice of opposition when Macie had ended things with Trent. Oh, how she wished she'd listened to the wise woman.

Collette's intervention gave Macie a much-needed reprieve, giving her time to collect her all-over-the-place thoughts. Well, as much of them as she could with Trent's hard stare anchored on her. What was he doing here? Could it be for the bachelor's auction? If so, why hadn't Mama Peaches mentioned it? Especially when Macie had volunteered to make sure all the bachelors were stage-ready.

The idea of Trent being one of the eligible bachelors filled her with unexplainable turmoil. She rested a gentle hand on her cartwheeling stomach, pulled in a long, deep breath, gave her system a much-needed reboot, then gingerly closed the gap between her and Trent. Shaken, she still flashed a smile as if his presence hadn't completely rocked her world off its axis.

"Hey," Macie said in a reserved tone when he and Collette parted. His steady gaze lit a blaze in her chest, the flame rising and scorching her cheeks, which she was sure were as bright red as a fire engine. After all of this time, why was she reacting to him this way? They were practically strangers.

"Hey," he said.

That voice. Low and deep. It felt like an eternity since she'd heard it. And crazy as it might have seemed, it calmed the frazzle inside of her.

"I have some things to do in the back. I'll let you two catch up," Collette said. "How long are you in town for, Trent?"

"Until Monday," he said.

"Maybe we can all get together for a drink before you leave," Collette said.

"Sounds good to me. It was great seeing you, Lette,"

Trent said.

"Same here."

Macie hadn't missed the look Collette tossed her as she disappeared into the back. Whatever the translation, Macie was sure something about second chances was there. In a foolish move—or maybe it was her way of trying to convince herself she was over him—Macie moved in for a hug. That was what strong women did, right? Showed their ex-lovers kindness? Attempted to convince them they weren't still pining over them? Displayed strength? Whether it was truly there or not.

Instantly, she was forced to banish the strangers assertion she'd mentally made earlier when the second she was in Trent's arms, something intensely familiar surged through her like a supercharged current. Through the layers of fabric between them, she felt his heart hammering in his chest. Or was it hers?

Their embrace lasted for what seemed like an eternity with neither one of them seeming overly eager to release the other. She couldn't recall the last time anything had felt so damn good against her body. Closing her eyes, she inhaled a lungful of his intoxicating fragrance. At that moment, she realized just how much she'd missed his manly scent, just how much she'd missed him.

Realizing she'd been clinging to Trent like a wet leaf to pavement, Macie released the fists full of his thick winter coat. She tried to step out of his arms, but his hold was still firm. As if realizing she was attempting to break free, his arms fell to his side and a troubled look strained his features.

Had he not wanted to let her go? Laughing to herself, she realized how ridiculous she sounded. She'd broken his heart. Other than hatred, she doubted he harbored anything for her, especially feelings.

So, why was he here?

Two

"So, what brings you to Chicago?" *Specifically, to my shop*, Macie wanted to add but kept to herself.

"The only women who could get me here," Trent said.

The only women who could get me here. Had he meant it as a jab to her? Had he wanted her to know his visit had absolutely nothing to do with his being in town? Truthfully, the proclamation saddened her a bit, but she tried not to let it show. "Ah. Mama Peaches. So, you are participating in the auction?"

Macie waited for a response, but Trent stared at her as if he hadn't registered a word she'd said. A second or two later, his head jerked like he realized she'd been speaking.

"I am. Um, Mama Peaches asked me to stop by and pick up the items she has here. She failed to mention you worked here."

Mama Peaches had sent him? She experienced a ping of disappointment by the fact he hadn't come on his own. It was a ridiculous notion to begin with. Why on earth would he have come to see her? "Own it, actually."

"Own it? That's great. Congratulations."

When they were younger, they'd always talked about owning their own businesses. That dream had come true for the both of them. Back then, their stories had always included each other. How they would always have each other's backs and be their biggest supporters.

"Thank you," she said, the memories of their plans paralyzing her momentarily.

A bout of silence fell between them, each eyeing the other as if trying to assess what—if anything—had changed about the other.

"You look…good," Macie said, breaking the uncomfortable silence. "Great, actually." And she wasn't kidding. Still those thick dark brows, strong jaw, full kissable lips.

"Thanks. So do you."

Did he really mean it, or was he just reciprocating? While he hadn't changed much, she had. Her once black hair was now a golden brown and her waist, hips and thighs were all a little thicker. Though, she believed she carried the extra pounds well.

"I guess married life agrees with you," Trent said.

It was faint, but Macie could have sworn Trent's jaw muscles tightened right before flashing a tight smile. Obviously, he'd heard she'd gotten engaged, but not that she'd called off the wedding two weeks before it was supposed to take place. "I wouldn't know. I'm not married."

Fine lines of confusion crawled along Trent's forehead. "I thought—"

"I called the wedding off," she said, cutting him off.

"Why?"

The question was so urgent, it startled Macie. And Trent seemed almost regretful he'd asked. There was no way she could confess she'd called off the wedding because it wasn't him she'd be marrying without sounding like a complete and utter fool. So, instead, she lied. "I don't think marriage is for me."

A slight wrinkle formed in Trent's brow. He was probably recalling the fact that when they were together, all she talked about was one day vowing her love to him on the pink sandy beaches of Horseshoe Bay in Bermuda. Unfortunately, their day in the sand never came.

"I guess Mama Peaches forgot to mention that, too," he said. "That you'd called off your wedding."

It seemed Mama Peaches had forgotten to mention a few things. Like the fact she'd had her best friend, Ms. Geraldine, pick up her dry cleaning over a week ago. Macie suppressed a laugh when she recalled Ms. Geraldine asking if the wig collection she treasured so much could be dry-cleaned. That woman would be buried with the adornments.

Her thoughts moved back to Mama Peaches. *What are you up to, sweet lady?*

"I guess I should grab the things and go," Trent said.

"Actually, they're not quite ready. One of the blouses has a stubborn stain I'm working to get out. I'll deliver them to her later."

Trent's brows furrowed. "Blouses? I thought she said quilts."

Shit. "Quilts?"

He nodded.

"Yes, that's what I meant. The blouses were last week. Um, the *quilt* has a stubborn stain. I, um, think that maybe Mama Peaches has been drinking Ms. Geraldine's homemade glory juice in bed. That stuff stains worse than red wine."

"Ah," he said.

Trent's stern expression revealed nothing, so she wasn't sure whether he'd believed her or not. She chose to think he had, despite knowing the man could always read her like a book, and probably knew she wasn't being truthful. Still, she maintained the best poker face she could muster.

"All right, then. I guess I'll be going."

He paused a moment, massaging the dusting of hair on

his cheek. God, that five o'clock shadow looked amazing on him.

"It was nice seeing you, Macie."

"You, too, Trent."

A second later, he turned and started away. Behind her, Macie heard Collette clear her throat. If she had to guess, the woman was trying to tell her not to let him get away.

"Would you like to grab a coffee?" Macie said, surprising herself by the invitation. "Mocha Books Café still has the best cappuccino around." His favorite.

Trent stopped just as his hand rested on the door, but it was a long second before he faced her. "No," he said.

Macie was certain the shock of his pointed rejection showed on her face. Without providing any explanation, he turned and continued out of the shop door. Not that he needed to. The reason was obvious. All the love he'd once felt for her had turned to hate. And who could blame him?

***

By the time Trent reached his rental car, he thought he'd pass out. Throwing himself into the driver's seat, he yanked out of his coat and tossed it aside, giving little regard to where the pricey piece landed. Despite the blistering thirty-eight degrees out, he was roasting. Was it an effect of seeing Macie? Of course, it was.

He held his hands out in front of him. They shook like those of a man facing an executioner. Trent's only crime was once loving Macie. A crime of the heart. One that had been punishable by sever torment.

He studied his reflection in the rear-view mirror. The short time he'd spent in Macie's presence had exhausted him. A part of him had wanted to accept her invitation. Another had wanted to get as far away from her as he could. Maybe she should have been on trial for the assault she'd caused on his body the second she stepped into his arms. It had been all he could do to release her. Nothing about that fact thrilled him.

Why in the hell had Mama Peaches failed to mention that Macie owned the cleaners? Well, the answer to that one wasn't hard to figure out. For one, she knew he would have never gone there. Two, the sly woman was playing matchmaker.

At least now he knew what she'd been holding back earlier at the house, that Macie wasn't married. He recalled the second their eyes had met when she'd rounded the corner. Stunned as hell, he hadn't been able to form a sentence. Neither could he stop staring at her.

Exquisite was the first thing that rumbled through his scattered brain. She wore the curve-hugging jeans and brown sweater well. Her unblemished brown skin glowed. Parts of her were a bit thicker than he remembered, but it made her that much more appealing to look at. Her hair had changed, even from the picture he'd seen at Mama Peaches'. Shorter. Lighter. It suited her perfectly. He couldn't deny that time had been damn good to her.

He relaxed against the icy leather seat of the sedan, his thrashing heart calming just enough for him to regain some semblance of composure. Was it normal for a woman to have this kind of effect on him? Especially one who'd crushed him. Fury ballooned inside him for responding to her this way.

Macie had ruined him. The few women he'd entertained over the years, he compared all to her, leading to relationship demise. One after another. He glared toward the shop, spotting Macie standing at the oversized glass window, staring out as if searching for something. Or someone. Him? Her head swept from one side to the other.

Even with the distance between them, he could feel her. Coursing through his body. Settling into his cells. Altering him. Clearly, she hadn't been as stuck on him as he had been on her. She'd moved on. Carried on with her life. Gotten engaged. Her coming close to becoming another man's wife angered him even more.

He wasn't exactly sure why she'd called off the wedding, but he damn sure knew it wasn't because she didn't think marriage was for her, as she'd stated. That lie he hadn't believed for one damn second. So, why?

Macie turned away from the window but instantly snapped her head back around. As if knowing exactly where to look, her eyes landed and locked on him. She rested a palm on the glass, her lips parted, then closed.

Fighting the strong bond that latched him to her, he dragged his gaze away, cranked the engine and drove away. All he had to do was avoid Macie for the next three days and he'd be home-free. Unfortunately, his gut told him it wouldn't be that simple.

Three

Macie sat at Mama Peaches' kitchen table, sipping hot tea with her and Ms. Geraldine, Mama Peaches' childhood friend. The two were inseparable. Apart, Mama Peaches and Geraldine were both a hoot. Together, they needed supervision. Mama Peaches could have been considered the more sound-minded one, while Ms. Geraldine took the term *no filter* to a whole new level. Both were characters and highly-respected in the neighborhood.

Macie couldn't help but smile as Mama Peaches gushed over her Gents and how happy she was that they would all be in town at the same time. When she'd stated some had resorted to kicking and screaming when they'd learned their roles, Macie wonder if one had been Trent.

"Send them my way. I'll sooth'em. They're grown men now. I can teach them a thing or two," Ms. Geraldine said.

Mama Peaches turned from the stove and rested a hand on her side. "Your hip bad. Your knee bad. Your back bad. Whatcha gon' teach'em? How to apply liniment?"

Macie nearly spit out her tea.

Ms. Geraldine rolled her eyes. "*Umph*. Grease me up,

and I'll run like a well-oiled engine for hours." She gyrated her hips in the chair. "Them young boys don't want known of this." She eyed Macie. "Ruin it for all you young girls."

The room filled with laughter.

When things calmed, Macie used the moment to broach the Trent thing. "I got a visit from one of your Gents yesterday." Of course, she wasn't telling Mama Peaches anything she didn't already know. "I was a little surprised to see him." More like stunned out of her mind.

Mama Peaches donned a look of confusion. "Did I not tell you Trent was coming to town?"

"No, ma'am." She was pretty sure she would have remembered that. But now that she thought about it, why hadn't she assumed he would?

"Lord, this old brain of mine. With so much going on, I guess I forgot to mention it."

"No, you didn't, Peaches," Ms. Geraldine said. "You're up to something. I can see that twinkle in your eyes."

"Hush up, Geraldine, 'fore I come snatch that purple wig off your head and drop it into this hot grease. Up in here looking like an unwrapped grape lollipop."

Considering the white pants suit and purple wig Ms. Geraldine wore, Macie agreed with the lollipop comment, but didn't voice it aloud.

Ms. Geraldine patted the side of her head. "I'll have you know this wig is hot."

"It looks hot. Hot as hell. And it's gon' be scorching hot come summertime."

"Not that kind of hot, heffa," Ms. Geraldine said. "*Stylish. Sexy.*"

Mama Peaches shook her head. "Chile, you a *hot* mess."

Macie imagined her and Collette identical to these two when they got older. Mama Peaches and Ms. Geraldine carried on. Mama Peaches condemned the gallery of wigs Ms. Geraldine owned, while Ms. Geraldine defended them, claiming they made her happier than any man ever had, and that she would be buried with her babies.

Ms. Geraldine's happy remark got Macie to thinking. Maybe she needed a wig, because she hadn't been happy in a long time. While Macie was daydreaming, Ms. Geraldine obviously said something hilarious, because Mama Peaches bent over with laughter.

"Go on, Geraldine. You ain't got a lick a sense in that wig-covered head of yours," Mama Peaches said, then turned to Macie. "Don't pay this one no mind. Ain't nobody up to nothing."

"*Mmm-hmm*," Geraldine hummed.

Mama Peaches clacked a pair of tongs at her.

"Do you still love him?" Ms. Geraldine asked.

"*Geraldine*! You know that ain't none of your business."

Ms. Geraldine scoffed. "Well, you the one trying to rekindle old flames. Might need to know if she even wants to be relit by him."

Macie expected Mama Peaches to protest again, but when she eyed the woman, she, too, appeared to be waiting for an answer. How did she respond? With a lie or the truth? "I—"

"Hello?"

All three women eyed the entryway to the kitchen. For Macie, that voice was unmistakable. Both her ears and her body recognized it. Trent. Tiny imaginary butterflies fluttered in her stomach. She sat a bit straighter and smoothed a hand over the pink cashmere sweater she wore.

"Guess we have our answer, Peaches," Ms. Geraldine said with a satisfied smirk.

"It smells good—"

Trent stopped mid-thought, his eyes colliding with Macie's and holding for a long while. The smile he'd entered with melted a little. Macie tried to convince herself that she wasn't the reason why, but she knew she had been. His distaste for her seemed to grow by the second.

While he still could turn heads in the black skull cap,

thick black jacket zipped to his chin, jeans, and mountain boots, he looked tired. The look was familiar, similar to ones she used to witness back in the day when stress made him restless, and he would toss and turn all night. Clearly, that hadn't changed.

When his attention left her—without so much as a nod in her directions—and settled on Ms. Geraldine, Macie released the breath she'd been strangling in her lungs, making sure it flowed out in a slow, steady stream and not a huge puff.

"Ms. Geraldine," Trent said, an affectionate smile curling his oh-so-kissable lips. He spread his arms and welcomed the several-inches-shorter woman into them. "It's good to see you," he said.

After several seconds of embracing, Ms. Geraldine pulled away and scrutinized him. "You looking well maintained. You got yourself a little southern belle taking care of you down there in Charlotte, North Carolina?"

Macie's breath hitched again. This time for a different reason. Anticipation. Though she truly wanted to hear his response, she couldn't believe Ms. Geraldine had asked the question. But now that it was out there...

Trent gave an unsteady laugh. "I see you're still a mess, Ms. Geraldine." He left her and moved to Mama Peaches.

Ms. Geraldine smiled and flashed Macie a thumbs up, which confused her. He'd cleverly avoided answering, which undoubtedly meant he was seeing someone. A wave of disappointment washed over Macie.

Of course he was seeing someone. What woman wouldn't snatch him right up. A successful, handsome, romantic—at least he had been when they had been together—man. *Had been* together. How could she have been so foolish? She'd sacrificed the best thing that had ever happen to her.

Trent deserved to be happy. And if this mystery woman made him happy, she was *happy-ish* for them.

She didn't get to be upset.

She didn't get to be sad.

She didn't get to be angry.

She didn't get to be jealous.

Losing Trent had been her fault, her bad decision, her punishment.

All of a sudden, the air in the room grew thick, and the walls felt as if they were closing in on her. Coming to her feet, she blurted, "I should go."

Mama Peaches and Trent stopped chatting and eyed her like she'd just yelled fire in a crowded room.

Ms. Geraldine rested her hand over her heart. "Chile, you done made me knock my wig crooked. You trying to give me a heartache? Yelling like you got that tonettes syndrome."

Macie was fairly certain she'd meant Tourette's.

"You stay. I'll go," Trent said.

For some unexplainable reason, Trent's words rubbed her the wrong way, and she lashed out at him. "Why does it sound like you think I'm leaving because of you?" Despite the fact that that was precisely why she was leaving; however, she would never admit that aloud. She continued, "I'm not some lovesick puppy feigning for a head rub from you, Trent."

Trent's expression hardened as if he were about to engage her. Then it softened like he'd reconsidered, like entertaining her was not worth his time. He gave Mama Peaches a kiss on the cheek and said, "I'll see you later," then gave Ms. Geraldine a parting hug.

A beat later, he left the room without so much as a sideways glance in Macie's direction. His coldness hurt like hell. Had she turned him into this heartless creature?

Macie inwardly chastised herself for acting so juvenile. Why couldn't she have simply kept her mouth shut?

"Huh," Ms. Geraldine said, eyeing the doorway. Facing Macie, she added, "Well, at least we know he still has feelings for you, too. That inferno dancing in his eyes told it all. Only a woman a man truly cares about can illicit such a reaction. I'm jealous."

Clearly, Ms. Geraldine needed to clean her glasses. If there had been fire in Trent's eyes, Macie was sure he would have shot flames at her.

Ms. Geraldine checked her watch. "Oh, shucks. I gotta run. I have a wig fitting." She said a hasty goodbye, grabbed her purse, and hurried out the room.

Macie turned to Mama Peaches. "He hates me."

"Hush that crazy talk," Mama Peaches said. "Geraldine was right about that inferno. There's clearly something he wanted—even needed—to say to you. But I taught all my Gents to be respectful, chivalrous, and above all else, honest. Maybe he felt you weren't ready for his truth." She neared Macie, wrapping an arm around her waist. "A lot of things are bucking around inside of that man, but hate ain't one of them. Not for you. I can promise you that."

How could Mama Peaches be so sure?

"For as much happiness as Southlake has brought him, it's delivered an equal amount of pain," Mama Peaches said.

"*I* brought him pain," Macie said, not necessarily for a response.

Mama Peaches gently rubbed a hand up and down Macie's back. "I won't lie. Yes, you did. But you also brought yourself a lot of pain. Sure, you've tried to mask it, but I see it. I see it because I see you."

Macie fought hard to hold back the tears threatening to fall, because Mama Peaches was so right. Her voice cracked when she spoke. "If I could just go back in time…"

"Chile, the past won't fix this. This is one knot that only the present can undo."

"He's…He's seeing someone," Macie said, the words bitter in her mouth.

"*Psshh.* That boy ain't seeing nobody. And if he is, he doesn't love her. He doesn't have that glow of a man in love. All I see on him is sadness, which makes me sad right along with him. You know the only time I believe I've ever seen him truly happy?"

"When?" Macie said, wiping a stray tear from her cheek.

"When he was with you." Mama Peaches smiled in that warm way that nurtured and soothed. "I do believe that was the last time I've seen you genuinely happy, too."

With that, Mama Peaches walked back to the stove before Macie could tell her how right she'd been.

***

Back in his hotel suite, Trent collapsed onto the mattress and released a tortured sound. At only two in the afternoon, he was already exhausted as hell. The unexpected encounter with Macie at Mama Peaches' place earlier had zapped his energy, just as the encounter with her at her business had. The visit to his mother's gravesite had further depleted him.

While the latter should have been more difficult, it hadn't been. What had been painstaking was another run-in with Macie. When he'd first walked in to see her sitting at the table, she'd taken his breath away. She'd looked so radiant in the pink sweater, updo, and light dusting of makeup.

Unfortunately, by the time he'd left, the euphoria had worn off. When she'd attacked him out of the blue with her words, he'd wanted to strike back, bring up every single syllable he'd been holding onto for so long. But he resisted. Still, he'd wanted to lash out at her so badly, he'd trembled.

Instead, he'd tamped down the lava-hot rage flowing through him and escaped. One thing Mama Peaches had always drilled into him was to be respectful, even if the person didn't deserve it, and that his peace of mind was far more important. One thing for certain, Macie had pushed him to the brink.

A feigning puppy. His jaw tightened. He'd assumed her aim at an abrupt departure had more to do with him than anything else, so he'd offered a solution. Clearly, it had been the wrong one. *No good deed goes unpunished.* Recalling the words often spoken by his mother quieted some of the angst inside him.

Bolting forward, he snatched his cell phone from the nightstand. Pressing the speed dial button associated with his business manager's phone number, he waited. Hopefully, she'd have some good news for him.

"You're supposed to be on a much-needed vacation, not calling me for status updates, which I'm certain is why you're calling," Brayden said, in lieu of a customary greeting.

Brayden knew him well. Too well, it seemed. He and Brayden had gone out on one date, but nothing ever materialized from it. They'd talked business most of the four hours. And by the end of the night, he'd offered her a job. They'd quickly discovered they were far more suited as boss and employee than lovers.

"How do you know I'm not phoning just to say hello?"

Laughter exploded from the opposite side of the line. Yep, she knew him.

"Any word on the deal?" He was in bidding to purchase an existing trucking company. It was a major move and undertaking, that honestly, scared him a little.

"Hopefully, soon," Brayden said.

"Good. No news is good news, I guess." He released a weighted sigh.

"Okay. What's up with you? You sound…strange."

"Nothing and everything," Trent said. Mostly everything. Mostly women. Mostly one woman in particular.

"Let me guess, Macie."

Brayden's assessment didn't surprise Trent. He'd shared bits and pieces of his past life in Chicago with her, including Macie and their breakup. "I don't want to talk about it," he said, somewhat defensively.

"You still love her. That's why she can still get under your skin."

"Love dried up for us a long time ago."

"I don't think so," she said. "You haven't been in a serious relationship since I've known you. I've watched women practically toss themselves at your feet, and you kicked them right back. You love her."

"I don't l—" For some reason, he couldn't finish the statement, and it irked the hell out of him. "Can we please change the subject?"

Brayden being Brayden, she ignored him. "Truthfully, I don't blame her for being hostile toward your ass."

Trent pulled the phone from his ear and eyed it like it was some kind of foreign object he'd never seen before. If anyone had a right to be hostile, it was him. Resting the device against his ear again, he said, "And why is that?" He wasn't the one who'd broken her heart.

"How do I put this gently." There was a brief pause. "You were an asshole for leaving her behind."

Trent's head snapped at her bluntness, though it shouldn't have surprised him. She'd never been one to hold her tongue. A small degree of anger bubbled up inside him. He wasn't to blame here, dammit. His tone was gruff when he spoke, "I didn't leave her behind. She abandoned *me*." He closed his lids tight, regretting sounding so weak. Softening his tone, he continued, "I had every intention of having her join me in North Carolina. I just needed to establish things first. I needed things to be perfect. *For her*. She was my queen. When I welcomed her there, I wanted her to walk into a castle, not a hobble."

"I bet all *she* wanted was you," Brayden said as calmly as a springtime breeze. "You told me how much you two loved one another. That she was your air."

"Yeah, and?"

"Well, if she was your air, you were probably her lungs."

Trent rested an elbow on his thigh, leaned forward and cradled his head in his hand.

Brayden's voice turned tender. "When a woman truly loves a man, Trent, truly loves him, we don't care about castles. We'll walk into anything, including a hobble, just as long as we're walking into it with him. It's as complicated and simple as that."

Trent wasn't sure how to respond. For the first time ever, he considered that maybe he had been selfish; wanted things on his terms; hadn't bothered to take into account what Macie wanted.

Now that he thought about it, maybe she had been trying to tell him in so many words that she hadn't cared that all he could afford at the time was a rundown one-bedroom in an unsavory part of town. But he had. He'd loved her. He had wanted her to be safe; wanted her to be happy; wanted her to be even more proud of him. Had wanted to show her how much she meant to him by securing a home for her, for them. Had he been wrong to ask her to wait on him while he took the time to build a sturdy foundation for them?

No, he hadn't. But as convinced as he was, Brayden's words flooded into his thoughts and rocked his psyche.

In an exhausted tone, he said, "I have to go, Bray. Keep me posted on the deal." He disconnected before she could respond. Tossing the phone aside, he kneaded his throbbing temple. It felt like someone was chipping away at it with an icepick.

He wasn't sure if he'd been right or wrong in his actions. All he knew was that now, he was more conflicted than ever. For so long, he'd blamed Macie, never once stopping to consider the role he'd inadvertently played in their split. He couldn't help but wonder if he had, would things have been different now?

Four

Macie arrived at the Southlake Park Cultural Center early to setup. Her task…make sure all tonight's bachelors were wrinkle-free and runway ready. She'd packed steamers, irons, sewing kits and anything else she might need to complete her job.

She'd always loved it here. From the sixty-four acres of pristine landscaping to its shoreline and rich history. Being here brought back a lot of good memories. Here was where she and Trent learned to draw and where a lost bet had resulted in a sulking Trent taking salsa lessons with her. Her eyes drifted to the culinary classroom where they'd been taught to make authentic Jamaican cuisine. But the most memorable visit here was when Trent had held her close and whispered he loved her for the very first time.

Whew. Macie released a heavy breath, batted her eyes to push back the tears, and continued through the building. She wasn't looking forward to facing Trent tonight. Not because she couldn't handle seeing him—she could, at least she hoped. It was because she was embarrassed by how she'd attacked him at Mama Peaches' place two days ago. Her cheeks burned, recalling her outburst.

The adult thing to do would be to apologize. However, she planned to simply avoid him instead. She had no other choice. Rational thinking eluded her when Trent was around. She couldn't afford to make herself resemble an even bigger nut by doing something completely preposterous tonight.

Macie's jaw dropped when she entered the grand ballroom, amazed at how the massive space had been transformed into something spectacular. Countless round tables, expensive linens, and exquisite centerpieces decorated the room. Highboy tables dotted with tea light candles and rose petals were randomly placed. The fact that donations had made this breathtaking scene possible warmed her heart.

The numerous floor-to-ceiling windows allowed an abundance of light to flood into the room, highlighting the impressive layout. A stage had been fashioned to spotlight the bachelors and accommodate the emcee. Men and women bustled about, putting what appeared to be the finishing touches on the room. This was surely going to be a night to remember.

Several hours later, the room being used for the behind-the-scenes work resembled backstage at a fashion show. Organized chaos. Expensive suits. Drop-dead gorgeous men. And enough sensual energy and confidence to overdose a rhinoceros.

Macie, along with Collette, worked feverishly attending to the men: steaming, adjusting neckwear, lint rolling. As good as these kings looked, this auction would secure truckloads of money.

As if drawn to do so, Macie paused mid-roll of a suit coat and glanced across the room, her eyes instantly locking with Trent's. Had he been watching her? He didn't smile, didn't frown, didn't turn away.

Their gazes held.

Teased.

Taunted.

Tantalized.

Tantalized?

Did his hard, awkward, unreadable stare actually entice her? Oh, God. It did. With this realization, the heat scorching her face burned a trail down her neck, blasted through her chest, swirled in her stomach and settled between her legs. She gasped and snatched her eyes away.

As planned, she'd avoided him. And up until this point, she'd done a good job of it.

***

Trent felt something.

Holding Macie's intense gaze, he felt something. Not anger. Not sorrow. Not malice. What was it? After several long seconds, Macie jolted, turned away, and continue lint rolling the suit jacket of some random dude he didn't recognize. But he was here, so he must have touched Mama Peaches' life in some way or vice-versa.

Desire.

That was what he'd felt latched on to Macie's gaze. Desire.

Pure.

Penetrating.

Preposterous.

Pleasantly soothing.

It had been so long since he'd felt such a clench that he'd barely recognized its all-consuming tug. But why now? This hadn't been his first encounter with Macie. Maybe it was the breakthrough Brayden had forced him to have.

Something occurred to him. This was the first time a wall of bitterness hadn't stood between them. What Brayden had said to him had stuck in the darkest recesses of his mind, taunting him relentlessly. He couldn't stop asking the question…*what if*. It was a paralyzing inquiry.

Still, it wasn't one he could so easily release from his thoughts.

A hand brushed over his shoulder. When he turned, he received another blast from his past. "Simone?"

Simone Battles smiled, revealing cosmetically straighten and whiten teeth. While the brown-skinned woman looked remarkably similar in the face as she had when he'd left town, her body had changed. Tremendously. He tried not to be too obvious in his scrutiny, but he was astonished by the transformation. She had to have lost over a hundred pounds.

"Trent Thatcher," Simone said.

Simone's silky voice reminded him of one of those adult phone operators he used to see advertising on late-night television. The red dress she wore was short, tight and revealed almost as much as her hungry perusal of his body. A smirk lifted one side of her mouth when her dark eyes found his again.

Feeling a bit uncomfortable, he shifted on his feet. "It's, um, been a long time, Simone. How have you been?"

Simone came in for a hug at the same time she answered, "Great. And by the look and feel of it, so have you."

Giving her a quick church hug, he pulled away. "Thanks."

"Maybe we—"

"Trent, there you are. It's your turn." The words came from behind him.

Trent glanced over his shoulder to see Collette, holding a lint brush in the air. Which confused him because she'd rolled him less than half an hour ago. Looking past her, he spotted something else, Macie's scowl. Before he could translate the meaning of the look, she was gone from the room, moving like a woman on fire.

"Mind if I steal him away for a moment, Simone." Collette said.

Simone's face went from sultry to sour. Her lips parted,

but Collette blocked whatever she was prepping to say.

"Thank you," Collette said, then all but dragged him across the room.

When Collette came to a stop, she pulled the littered sheet off the spool, then rolled him again. Hard.

"Um, Collette, is everything okay?"

She stopped abruptly. "*Um*, no," she said glowering at him.

"Did…I do something?" Trent asked, unsure what he could have possibly done to cause a usually mild-mannered Collette to act this way.

"Did he do something?" she mumbled to herself. "Well, first you roll back into town and throw my best friend's world off balance. Then you treat her like crap. And as if that wasn't enough, you're over here flirting with the one woman you know Macie despises." Her tone softened considerably. "Are you intentionally trying to hurt her?"

She stormed away before he could answer.

What the hell just happened? Trent pushed his brows together so hard it hurt. *Intentionally, trying to… Shit. Renzo.* On his life, he hadn't even considered the bad blood between Macie and Simone. Macie had blamed Simone for her cousin's wrongful incarceration when the woman had made him an accessory to a robbery her trifling boyfriend, at the time, had been responsible for.

He shot a glance in the direction Macie had moved. Had she thought…? Did she think…? *Shit.* An urge to run after her nearly overtook him, but he stayed rooted to the floor. Why was he so concerned about hurting Macie? She hadn't been worried about hurting him.

Still, her probable perception of the situation bothered him. And that pissed him off. The sooner he returned to North Carolina, the better.

***

"I'm fine," Macie said, attempting to convince Collette that seeing Trent with Simone hadn't bothered her, when, in fact, it had. How could he? He knew how she felt about the woman.

Redirecting her thoughts, she focused on dressing for thc auction. The royal blue evening gown would make her feel better. She'd paid an insane amount for the designer dress, but the skew neck, high-waisted mermaid piece hung from her body like a priceless work of art hung in a museum. Perfectly.

Who knows, maybe she'd even bid on one of the eligible bachelors, take him home and screw out all of her frustrations. She laughed. As if she were that bold. Or scandalous.

"What's so funny?" Collette asked. "Oh, God. You're not having some kind of breakdown, are you? I'm not sure I can handle it in this dress."

If Jeremy could see Collette now in the maroon-colored, curve-hugging, sparkly gown, he'd walked across the water to get to her. "No, silly. I'm just…" She glanced heavenward. "I'm just finally getting on with my life. I'm going to respond to some of the invitations I've received from my online dating profile. I better not get hacked up by some psycho. If I do, I'm going to haunt you for eternity."

"Deal," Collette said.

A half an hour later, Macie sat in the audience with several dozen eager women, holding a bidding paddle she didn't intend to use. Occupying her table were Collette, Mama Peaches, Ms. Geraldine, and four additional women she recognized from the community center where she volunteered Wednesday nights teaching adult reading classes.

Macie could feel someone's eyes on her, so she scanned the room, landing on Simone. The heffa had the nerve to smile at her. Well, not as much a smile as it was a cunning sneer.

"Did that heffa just sneer at you?" Collette leaned in to ask.

"Yep." Macie rolled her eyes away from the harlot. Downing the remainder of the champagne in her flute, she collected another from the passing tray, finishing it in two gulps.

"Okay, ladies, leave that swamp water alone. I brought something special for us to enjoy," Ms. Geraldine said. She removed a bottle from her oversized purse. "Glory juice. Who wants some?"

"I do," Macie said, passing Ms. Geraldine her empty glass. "Fill'er up." While she wasn't much of a drinker, she needed something to lull her spirit.

Collette passed her glass, too. "Might as well."

Mama Peaches declined. "None for me. The last time I partook of that concoction in public, I wound up grinding with old man Juniper. Guess I put too much grind into it 'cause I had to threaten that fool with my Henrietta to make him stop showing up at my front door uninvited. No, thank you."

Henrietta was Mama Peaches' nine-millimeter handgun she carried with her everywhere.

"Suit yourself," Ms. Geraldine said. "But I'm about to get lit."

Macie took several small, cautionary sips of the burgundy-colored beverage. It didn't taste that strong. Rather smooth, actually. With a nice after-warmth. This was just what she needed.

The emcee called for everyone's attention, then announced the commencement of the auction. Hungry women readied themselves for the first bachelor who would grace the stage, straightening in their seats, paddles at the ready.

When bachelor number one strolled out, struck a pose, and flashed a dazzling smile, the crowd went mad. Macie simply took another sip from her glass. Right now, the glory juice was giving her more pleasure than the man on the stage.

By bachelor number twenty-three, Macie was well in the grasp of Ms. Geraldine's homemade wine. She leaned over and tapped Collette on the shoulder. "*Collette,*" she whispered. "*Collette,*" she said again, but this time much louder. When Collette faced her, Macie grinned and said, "I love you. You're the bestest best friend ever."

"I love you, too, girl," Collette said.

A blink later, both women burst into laughter.

Macie reached for her glass, but Mama Peaches confiscated it. "Hey," Macie said.

"Oh, I think you've both had enough," Mama Peaches said, securing Collette's glass, as well. "Geraldine, I told you to stop plying them. Look what you done done. Got'em both high as Mount Everest."

Ms. Geraldine gave a wobbly smile, clearly tipsy herself.

"I love you, too, Mama Peaches," Macie said. "You're the best Mama Peaches in the whole wide world. Thank you for being there when my parents died. And I love you…" She pointed to Ms. Geraldine. "And you..." This one directed at the community center lady number one. She jabbed a finger to lady number two, three and four. "And you, and you and you." She swept her arm around the room. "I love everybody. But I really love—"

Macie stopped mid-thought when the emcee announced that coming to the stage was The Carolina Bandit. "*Carolina Bandit?*" she mumbled to herself. Her eyes landed on Trent, floating across the stage like a heavenly deity. She sucked in a sharp breath, the rush of air sobering her some. "He's magnificent," she said to no one in particular.

When the bidding started, Macie's hand inched dangerously close to her own paddle. Trent worked the stage like a pro. Unfastening his jacket, he flashed a mischievous grin. The sea of lady piranhas ate it up.

Every move he made seemed to thrill them more: sliding his hands into his pockets, pulling them out.

Folding his arms across his chest, unfolding them to rest at his sides. Striking a pose, unstriking it to roam the stage. It was all so overwhelming.

Trent stopped and scanned the crowd with a narrow-eyed gaze. The expression on his face was one of the most dangerous, most arousing, most commanding looks she'd ever seen him don. Her stomach quivered with excitement—along with other things. Remembering how his large hands used to roam all over her body, igniting a blaze that seared every inch of her, made her nipples bead in her bra. God, she really needed a hit of glory juice right now.

The bids hit a thousand, then two thousand, then three thousand dollars. These women were serious. Subconsciously, Macie's hand tightened around the wooden paddle handle, then relaxed it, resting it in her lap.

"Four thousand dollars," came from several tables away.

Macie went rigid at the sound of the familiar voice. She searched, finally locating the source. Simone Battle. Macie growled under her breath at the woman and the satisfied expression on her face. A notion to sprint across the room and snatch that alpaca wig off her head was nearly too much to resist. But she did.

"We have four thousand," the emcee said, drawing Macie's attention from the farm animal atop Simone's head and back to the stage. "Four thousand. Can we get forty-five hundred."

There was a lot of whispers in the room. Macie assumed the women were trying to figure out if they could afford the high cost or debating whether or not Trent was even worth it. Obviously, someone thought he was.

"Forty-five," came from the opposite side of the room.

Macie's eyes settled on the young lady flashing her paddle like a guiding light for aircraft. The woman's expression was more self-gratifying than Simone's had been.

"Forty-Five. Can I get Five thousand? Five thousand? Anyone?"

Clearly, Simone had wanted Trent, but obviously not five thousand dollars worth of him, because the sour-faced woman tossed her paddle aside and gulped whatever was in her glass.

"Okay, forty-five hundred going once. Forty-five hundred going twice. G-"

"Five thousand!"

"Atta girl," Ms. Geraldine said.

Macie glanced at Ms. Geraldine, confused by her words. "Huh?" It only took her a second to realize she was standing. Then another to filter into her head that she'd bid on Trent. *Oh, God.* She'd bid on Trent. Wanting to dart from the room, her feet were cemented to the floor.

The emcee called for higher bids. None came. When the gavel banged on the podium, and the emcee announced, "Gone," the enormity of what had just happened sank into every cell in Macie's body. But for some reason, hearing the roaring applause, a bloom of satisfaction blossomed in her chest, her lips ticking up into a nervous smile.

Then she made the mistake of tracing her eyes back to the stage. Her false bravado wore off the second she locked gazes with Trent. The room suddenly grew boiling hot. And it quavered, like someone was outside rocking the building. What in the hell had she done?

Trent's expression: emotionless.

Stare: unyielding.

Stance: rigid.

He was either angry as hell or stunned stupid.

Five

Backstage, Trent washed a hand over his head. What in the hell had just happened? Obviously, he knew what had just happened. Macie had placed a bid on him and had won. He just couldn't believe it. While she'd been the first thing he'd seen when he stepped onto the stage, looking more radiant than usual, she was the last person he would have ever expected to raise her paddle.

While the situation wasn't funny, he couldn't help but chuckle, recalling how she'd darted to her feet, visibly unsteady. Had she been drinking? No. Macie rarely drank. Well, the Macie he'd known rarely drank. Who knew what she did now.

Five thousand dollars. Apparently, the dry-cleaning business was a cash cow. He rested a hand on his hip, lowered his head, and massaged the tightness in his neck with his free hand. *So much for avoiding her.* How was he going to get out of this one? *Mama Peaches.* She would understand why he couldn't spend an evening with Macie, right? Of course, she would. Problem solved.

"What an interesting turn of events," came from behind him.

Trent turned to see Mama Peaches approaching. Just the person he needed to see. "I'd say."

Mama Peaches patted him on the cheek. "Let me guess. You're back here trying to figure out how to get out of spending time with her. Am I right?"

No doubt she knew she was right, but Trent nodded anyway. "Any suggestions?"

"Just one," Mama Peaches said. "Stop running."

Before he could respond, someone summoned Mama Peaches. She flashed him one of her warmth-filled smiles and strolled away.

So much for Mama Peaches' help. Trent left the room. When he found Macie, he'd simply tell her that their spending time together was not a good idea. No running. Just the plain and simple truth. He paused. What if she asked why? It was Macie. Of course, she would. But he didn't owe her any explanations.

On his quest to find her, he cursed under his breath, "*Dammit.*" Why had she bid on him? And what had she expected from placing that bid. That they would hangout like old friends? Reminisce? Catch up? What? She had to know it wouldn't have been that simple. If her feelings got hurt from what he intended to say to her, it would be her own damn fault.

As he headed toward the ballroom, Trent worked it all out in his head. He would reimburse her the five thousand dollars, get in his car and hightail it back to his hotel room. Instead of Monday, he would return home tomorrow. He'd definitely had enough of Southlake.

When his cellphone rang, he stopped. Brayden's name showed. Swiping his thump across the screen, he made the call active. "Hello?"

"I need you," she said.

"Umm…"

"Oh, please. I don't need you like that. Just like a man to make it sexual. I need you here. Back in North Carolina. Tomorrow."

That worked out well because he'd planned to be back in North Carolina tomorrow. But he didn't share that with Braden. She probably would have accused him of running, too. "What's the urgency?"

"Well," she said casually, "someone has to sign these intent papers. And since my name isn't Trent Thatcher…"

"Wait. Intent papers? Does that mean what I think it means?"

"Yes, it does. Congratulations, you've just acquired your first of many new fleets."

Trent pressed his lids tight and pumped his fist into the air. *Yes*, he mouthed quietly.

"You did it," Brayden said.

"*We* did it," Trent corrected her.

"Okay, we did it."

He could hear Brayden's smile in her voice.

"Now get your ass back to North Carolina. I want to get the papers signed asap. I don't want anything holding up finalizing this deal. I want it out of our office and in theirs first thing Monday morning."

"Aye aye, captain. I'll be there," Trent said, ending the call.

Trent entered the ballroom, instantly homing in on Macie by the bar with Chavis Durant. She didn't look overly joyed by his presence. No doubt he was trying to run some kind of lame game on her. He had always disliked Durant. A pompous, arrogant, self-absorbed bastard who used his family's money as a crutch.

"Chavis Durant," Trent said, interrupting whatever was happening here.

Chavis lazily faced Trent, regarding him like an unwelcome disturbance. A smug expression spread across the man's face, his pond water green eyes twinkling with mischief. "Trent Thatcher. Long time."

Not long enough, Trent thought. He could have gone a lifetime without ever seeing the man. Trent slid his attention to Macie. Her glassy eyes, flushed face, and dazed look suggested she'd had a little too much to drink. The thought of Chavis preying on her filled him with rage. "Can we talk?" he asked Macie.

Macie regarded him blankly for several seconds. "S-sure," she said, her words slow and choppy.

When Macie attempted to move away, Chavis took her hand and kissed the back. Trent's fists tightened at his sides. *She's not yours*, he reminded himself, and slowly relaxed his tense muscles.

Chavis flashed a wicked grin. "I'll be waiting for you," he said.

Macie snatched her hand away and silently moved on. Something told Trent that Chavis would be waiting a long time. And by the letdown expression on Chavis' face, he knew it, too.

Trent knew he should have simply walked away, but he felt an overwhelming need to pour salt into Chavis' wound. He shrugged one shoulder. "Better luck next time, I guess."

"There's always tomorrow." Chavis smirked, then moved on to his next target, a busty brunette who appeared eager to entertain the clown.

"Asshole," Trent mumbled, then moved behind Macie.

Macie swayed when she turned to face him. "*Oops*," she said, her eyes wide, clearly startled by his closeness.

Without thinking, he reached out to steady her, resting his hands on either side of her waist. "Whoa."

Macie gripped his forearms and shivered. "Thank you." Her eyes lowered and lingered on his mouth. "That was very kissable of you." She tossed her head back and gave a silly laugh. "I said kissable, didn't I?"

"Yes."

She laughed so more. "I meant *kind*. Kind, kind, kind. That's what you are. Kind."

"Have you been drinking?" he asked, the answer obvious. Plus, he could smell the alcohol on her breath.

Her eyes widened. Stumbling out of his hold, she

shook her head adamantly, causing her to sway again. This time, he kept his hands to himself. Luckily, she didn't topple over.

"No?"

Her response sounded more like a question than a comment.

"Well, yes. But no, not really. I mean, I've been *drinking*, yes. But not *drinking, drinking*. Not like *drunk* drinking."

Trent folded his arms across his chest and studied her with narrowed eyes as she kept brushing at something on her neck that wasn't actually there. It was all he could do to not laugh as she rambled on and on about how *not* drunk she was.

Finally, she released an exhausted sigh. "Yes. Yes, I've been drinking. And I might be a little," she pinched her thumb and forefinger together, "drunk. But not—"

"Drunk, drunk," he said, finishing her statement.

She flashed a triumphant grin. "Exactly. I'm on vacation next week. I'll sleep it off."

Realizing whatever was told to her tonight, she probably wouldn't remember tomorrow, he said, "Let me take you home."

"You don't need to. I drove," she said.

"Really?" he said. "Oh, okay. Can I see your keys?"

"I don't know, can you?" She laughed as if she told the best joke of her life. "That was a good one," she said, fishing inside her clutch. She dangled the keys in the air. "Here they are."

Trent took them from her and slid them into his pocket.

"Hey," she said.

"Come on. Let's get you home."

Before leaving, Trent found Mama Peaches attempting to wrangle Collette and Ms. Geraldine, who both appeared just as wasted as Macie. When he informed Mama Peaches he was driving Macie home, she grinned wide enough to crack the corners of her mouth. Clearly, she had read far too much into his kind gesture. He simply didn't want Macie wrapping her car around a tree on his conscience.

Ten minutes into the drive, Macie was fast asleep. Trent watched her a second or two. Even in her peaceful slumber, she was beautiful. A warm sensation swirled in the pit of his stomach. He shouldn't be here. Not with her.

Rolling his eyes back to the road ahead, he sighed. *Get her inside and leave.* Simple as that. So, why didn't it feel uncomplicated?

"Why are you being nice to me, Trent?" she asked in almost a whisper. "You hate me. And you should. I'm an awful person. I did an awful thing to you. To us. I'm sorry."

"Macie—" When he glanced over, her eyes were still closed, lips parted, and she snored lightly. "I don't hate you," he said, mostly for his own benefit. And that was part of the problem.

After a slow effort, Trent and Macie finally made it to the front door of her ranch-style home. Helping Macie into one of the white rockers, he imagined her on the porch, sipping tea and reading a book by her favorite romance author. Shaking his head, he scattered the comforting image.

Trying several keys, he finally got one to slide into the lock. After cracking the door, he got Macie back to her feet.

"Make sure you lock the door. I don't want him to get in."

Didn't want him to get in? Obviously, she referred to that asshole Chavis.

"I'm so tired," she said.

A sweet scent greeted him the second they stepped inside. Macie had always loved her plug-in air fresheners. The spacious home was decorated in an array of warm browns and bold purples. The modern décor suited her.

"Where's your bedroom?" he asked.

Macie kicked off her shoes. "In my bedroom, silly."

Trent laughed. "Okay, which is where?"

Macie trudged down the hall, tugging at her dress. "Can you help me get out of this thing? It's so heavy. And hot."

"I'll help you. Let's just get to your bedroom first," he said.

"'Kay."

Macie's bedroom was a deep teal and cream color-scheme, accented with mahogany furniture. A cream tufted fabric club chair with ottoman sat in one corner. A teal throw and book resting in it. The space screamed ultra cozy.

"I have to pee," Macie said, attempting to free herself again.

"Wait a second," Trent said. She continued to struggle, so he put a little more bass in his voice when he said, "Macie." When she looked at him with those innocent-looking brown eyes, he added, "Wait a second."

"'Kay," she said.

"Turn around." When she did, Trent lifted his hands but paused before making contact with the fabric.

"I gotta go now," Macie said, rushing toward a closed door.

Trent blew a sigh of relief when she disappeared inside. Every cell in his body warned him that being here was a bad idea. Now would be the perfect time to make his getaway. He'd done what he'd set out to do, making sure Macie was safe inside her home.

She was.

So why was he still standing here?

Something clattered inside the bathroom, startling him from his thoughts. He inched a couple of steps closer to the door. "You okay in there?"

"No. My hair…is struck," she said.

Trent pushed his brows together. *Stuck*? He washed a hand over his head. "I'm coming—" Before he could finish his thought, Macie stepped out. Trent's brows arched. "Whoa."

She'd obviously attempted to… Hell, he had no idea what she'd been attempting to do. A pink, wide-toothed comb was tangled in her hair, dangling in front of her face. The once neatly-styled updo now resembled a wiry honeycomb.

The comparison made him recall the nickname he'd given her years ago. *Bumblebee.* His Bumblebee. Because she'd buzzed into his life and turned everything sweet. Abandoning the past, he said, "Let me help you."

"'Kay," she said.

Trent stepped forward and worked the plastic up and down, right and left. How in the hell had she managed this?

"*Ouch*," she said in a whine.

"Sorry." He continued to unthread strands from the teeth.

Macie inhaled a deep breath. "You smell good."

"Thanks."

"You're welcome." She yawned. "I'm so tired. Can't you just cut it out?"

Trent laughed. "You probably wouldn't be too pleased with me in the morning. I've almost…" A second later, he pulled the offending comb free. "…got it."

Macie's once sleepy eyes lit with excitement. "Thank you."

Without warning, she came up on her tiptoes and pecked him on the lips, a tender kiss that made his entire mouth tingle for more. He fought it as hard as he could. *It* being the craving to taste her more thoroughly, more completely. He knew that was the last thing he needed to do.

But he did it anyway.

This kiss was like sunshine and rain.

Thunder and calmness.

Lightning and blue skies.

A cleansing breath and a vice clenching his lungs.

It was all of those things, all at once. He needed to pull away, wanted to pull away from this furious storm of desire threatening to wash him out to sea and drown him in a tidal wave of arousal.

Parts of him that should have remained dormant came to life, torturing him with a painful erection. His heart pounded in his chest, threatening to crack his rib cage. He wanted Macie. Wanted her in a way that defied all understanding, even his own. Maybe even needed her. It had been so long since he'd experienced the kind of pleasure she'd once been able to bring him. And by the way his body spun out of control, he knew she still could.

Somehow, he mustered the strength to pull away from temptation. His breathing was ragged and unstable. Blood whooshed in his ears, making it hard for the voice of reason to seep through.

Macie's lips remained puckered and eyes closed for several seconds. When they finally opened, she touched her lips. "Was that real?"

"No," he said. But truth was, it was the realest thing he'd felt in three years. "Come on. Let me help you to bed," he said, and led her from the room.

"It felt real," she mumbled.

With shaky hands, he fumbled with a clasp on her dress, then a button, then the zipper. His breath seized in his chest when the fabric pooled at her feet, revealing her smooth, brown skin and the sexiest dark gray panty and bra set he'd ever seen. Sparkles and lace. His fingers ached to touch her, so he did. But only long enough to direct her into bed. He made a motion to cover her, but she pushed up on her elbow.

"I can't sleep in this thing," she said.

Before he had an opportunity to react, she removed her bra and tossed it across the room, then fell back onto the mattress. He covered her quickly. But despite his urgency, he'd gotten a glimpse of the breasts that had once fit so perfectly in his hands.

Macie's eyes closed the second her head touched the pillow. Easing down on the edge of the bed, he brushed several stray strands of hair from her forehead and eyed her for several seconds. "Goodbye, Macie Shaw."

She stirred when he stood. When she didn't open her eyes, he moved away.

"Don't leave me, Trent. Not again. Please. I still l…" Her words trailed as she apparently drifted off to sleep again.

Frozen in the spot where he stood, Trent's chest tightened at what she'd said, and had not said.

Six

The sound of the ringing phone caused Macie to bolt forward in bed and glance around as if she had no idea where she was. Her location registered a couple of seconds later. *Home.* She was home. But how did she get here? And why couldn't she remember?

Scrambling for the receiver, she pressed the cold plastic to her ear and fell back onto the mattress. "Hello," she said, barely recognizing her own croaky voice.

"Are you awake?" Collette asked. "And alone?" She chuckled.

"Why are you screaming?" Macie kneaded her fingers into her pounding temple. "Yes, I'm awake. And why wouldn't I be alone? What time is it?"

"One o'clock."

Macie panicked. Calls at this hour of the morning usually signaled one thing, someone was dead or close to it. The thought sent a wave of panic through her, causing her head to throb even harder and her stomach to churn. "What's wrong? Is everything okay?"

"Huh?" Collette said.

"People only phone at one in the morning when

something is wrong. Now what is it?"

Collette laughed. "Sweetie, it's one in the *afternoon*, not the morning."

"One in the…" Macie cracked one eye and sought the clock on her nightstand, then sent a glance toward the window. A tiny stream of light filtered through her blackout curtains. Light that wouldn't be present at one in the morning. "I'm so confused," she said. Macie raked through her memory. The night before was a blur. "What happened last night? How did I get home?"

"Ms. Geraldine's glory juice. And the open bar. You got wasted."

Wasted? But I don't drink. At least not enough to result in a hangover. She groaned. A serious hangover. "I never drink like that."

"Well, baby doll, you did last night."

"And you let me?"

Collette laughed. "I wasn't exactly in a position to run interference. I sipped the juice, too."

"How did I get home?" Macie asked again.

"Trent drove you."

Macie's eyes popped open. "Trent?" Now Collette's earlier *alone* statement made sense. Her eyes swept the room. No sign of him. Why would Trent, of all people, drive her home? Had he volunteered, or had Mama Peaches instructed him to?

"Yes. I guess he didn't want anything to happen to you," Collette said. "And…I guess now would be a good time to tell you that you placed the winning bid on him at the auction."

Obviously, Collette hadn't consumed as much alcohol as she had, because the woman seemed to be a wealth of information. And the information was getting crazier and crazier by the minute. "*I* bid on Trent?" What in the hell was in Ms. Geraldine's glory juice?

"Yes, *you* did. Five-thousand-dollars, to be exact."

"*Five-thousand dollars*!" Macie ignored the pain that shot

through her forehead. The temperature in the room rose to what felt like a hundred degrees. Using what energy she could muster, she tossed the covers back. A second later, she released a sound between a gasp and a screech.

"What's wrong?" Collette asked, concern present in her tone.

Did she chance telling Collette she wasn't wearing a bra? That would probably just lead to more questions she couldn't answer. "Um, n-nothing." The dress she'd worn was neatly folded and draped over the armrest of her reading chair, along with her bra. Something told her she hadn't done that, which meant Trent had. Closing her eyes, she said a quick prayer that she hadn't made a fool of herself. Again.

"Are you still there?" Collette said.

Macie swung her legs over the side of the bed. "Yes. Can I call you back? I really need to take something for the wicked headache." What she really needed to do was figure out what the hell happened last night. Obviously, she couldn't ask Trent because he'd clearly hightailed it out of there.

"Okay. Love you, girl."

"Love you, too," Macie said, then ended the call.

Macie sat on the side of the bed and summoned memories of the night before. Some came back to her in bits and pieces. Arriving at the cultural center. Using the steamers and lint rollers. A blurry vision of several men roaming the stage flashed in her head, their faces askew.

Groaning, she pushed to her feet, gathering her equilibrium before moving into the bathroom. Catching a glimpse of herself in the mirror, she shrieked. *What the…?* She combed her fingers through the mass of unruliness atop her head.

Dismissing the exhausting task, she studied her reflection. She could send a scarecrow running for cover. Clumped mascara, smudged eyeliner, smeared lipstick. She dragged her thumb over her bottom lip.

Taking the quickest shower in history, she slid into a pair of comfortable granny panties and an oversized purple night shirt. Her first instinct was to climb back into bed, but the need to quench her ravenous thirst won out.

She stopped dead in her tracks when light blossomed in the hallway. The backdoor. Her breathing seized and she couldn't move a muscle. Bile burned the back of her throat, and she felt lightheaded. That terrifying night three years ago thrashed around in her head. *Not again. It couldn't be happening again.* Her brain seized, totally confused about what to do next. The hallway dimmed as the door creaked closed. *Run, Macie.* The tiny voice in her head did little to urge her legs forward.

Macie's throat thickened with pure fear. She waited, panicked, stared helplessly at the large shadow growing closer and closer. Then, it was there. Somehow, she managed a scream. Strong arms wrapped around her and she fought to free herself.

"Macie, it's me."

The commanding voice filtered through her delirium. "T-Trent?" His face slowly came into focus. Her chest heaved and legs wobbled, threatening to betray her at any moment.

A weary smile played on Trent's face as he stared down at her. "Yes. Damn, woman. You scared the hell out of me."

Her lips parted, but her brain was too scrambled to speak. His brows furrowed, and she recognized genuine concern on his face.

"You're trembling," he said.

Finally able to form a sentence, she said, "I'm fine." She tried to free herself from his embrace, but his grip remained. Staring into his eyes, she recognized that grilling gaze. He didn't believe her.

"I'm fine, Trent." Despite what she'd claimed, she wasn't fine. But there was no way she would tell him what she'd gone through. "What are you still doing here?"

While being in Trent's arms gave her a sense of security, a flood of terror still coursed through her. His arms finally fell, and she reluctantly left his hold. Unable to maintain their intense connection, her eyes drifted away from his.

His crisp white shirt hung on the outside of his suit pants. The expensive fabric clung to his upper arms, highlighting the contours of his biceps. His loosened bowtie dangled around his neck. When she realized she was biting at her bottom lip, she jolted. "Um, what did you say you were still doing here?" she asked.

"You were pretty out of it. I was worried you would get up and try to cook or something. You're stubborn like that." A corner of his mouth curled slightly. "I figured I'd better hang around."

While his explanation had flowed smoothly and rang authentic, she had her doubts that it was the real—or at the very least, the whole—reason he'd stayed. Trent still had a tell. Whenever he wasn't being wholly truthful with her, he'd massage the left side of his jaw, similar to how he was doing now. So, what was he withholding?

"Thank you for your concern," she said. "I need something to drink." She moved into the kitchen and Trent followed.

"Drink this. It'll make you feel better."

Macie's face scrunched at the brownish liquid in the glass he offered. Taking it, she studied the contents with a keen eye. "What is it?"

"Fresh ginger, water, honey and lemon juice."

"Thank you, but no, thank you." She smiled and passed it back to him. "I'll just grab some coffee."

Refusing to take it back, he said, "Coffee's a diuretic. You need liquids."

She lifted the glass to her nose and took a whiff. It didn't smell all that bad. The least she could do was take a sip, since he'd gone through the trouble of preparing it. "*Mmm*," she hummed.

"Swallow it, Macie."

Dang it. Forcing her throat muscles to work, she was pleasantly surprised. The concoction definitely didn't taste as unappetizing as it looked. Actually, it was quite refreshing. She took several more sips. "Not bad."

"Told you." Trent looked away briefly. "I, um, hung around for another reason," he said.

Setting the glass on the counter, she said, "Okay."

"Unfortunately, I can't stick around long enough to satisfy my obligation to you. For placing the winning bid," he said as if for clarification. "I have an urgent issue back home."

Wow. He was getting really good at blowing her off. First the coffee invitation. Now this. Well, if he was this determined to blow her off that he had to make up an excuse to get out of it, she wouldn't challenge him. So be it. Conjuring the warmest smile she could under the circumstances, she said, "I understand." He looked bemused by her response.

"I'm finalizing an important deal."

Why did it sound as if he was trying to explain himself to her? He owed her nothing, especially an explanation. She nodded. "Okay."

His brows crinkled slightly, then relaxed. What had he expected? That she would be distraught and beg him to stay? No way. She could take a hint.

"I'll reimburse you the money you spent," he said.

"That won't be necessary, Trent. I did it for a good cause." She gulped the rest of the liquid to ease the nausea brought on by the fact she'd just turned down his offer. She could cover it, but it would definitely take a bite out of her savings. She'd toyed with getting away for a few days since she was on vacation all week, but that was out the window now.

"Thank you for making sure I got home safely. That was kind of you," she said, struggling to keep her disposition sunny.

"And saving you from Chavis Durant."

Saving her from Chavis Durant? Confused, she said, "What does that mean?"

Trent gave a strained chuckled. "I'm fairly certain he'd wanted a little alone time with you."

Macie knew exactly what Trent meant by alone time. Chavis Durant was a pig she wouldn't have wasted any amount of her time on. Normally. But nothing about the night before had been normal. Her stomach flip-flopped at the idea of what could have happened. How could she have been so stupid? "Thank you." Her voice was low and laced with shame. She was never drinking again.

A thick veil of silence descended on them as they stared one another down. Unmistakable energy flowed between them. She could feel it. Could he? Of course, he could. It was too powerful to ignore. Heat scorched her neck and rose to her cheeks.

"I should go," Trent said, interrupting their zing. "I have a plane to catch."

"Oh. Um…okay. Don't want to miss your plane and be stuck here. In Chicago, I mean. I'm sure you're eager to return home. That important deal and all." But was that truly the reason? Was it work or a woman he was returning to? Silently, she chastised herself for even caring.

Macie led Trent toward the front of the house. "It was good seeing you, Trent." And she truly meant it. There was far more she wanted to say to him, and far more she would have said to him, had she thought he cared to hear it. "Take care of yourself."

Trent flashed her a weary smile. "You do the same."

"I will." She closed the door then butted her back against it. A moment later, she veered into the living room and peeped out of the blinds just in time to see him getting inside a black sedan. "Goodbye, Trent Thatcher," she mumbled, countless emotions swirling inside her.

Allowing the slats to fall back in place, she closed her eyes to gather her thoughts. A snippet of last night filled her head, causing her to draw in a sharp breath. Her eyes snapped opened, and she pressed two fingers to her lips. They'd kissed.

Closing her eyes again, she forced more to come. An astonishing reel began to play, the images as clear and crisp as a November sky. The recall rocked her to the soul. Butterflies fluttered in her stomach, and she pushed her palm against her mid-section to calm the movement. Then, as if it had reached its end, the scenes faded, and her memory bank went dark.

"No," Macie said, reaching out as if she could secure the dimming flashes in her hand.

They'd kissed.

The doorbell sounded, startling her. She made her way back to the door and pulled it open. The frigid air blew in like a vulture claiming its prey. She shivered, then cradled her body with her arms. "Trent? Did you forget something?"

Trent stood silent for a moment, his lips parting slightly. A white tendril of heated air floated between them. "Come with me."

***

Trent stole several glimpses of Macie as they drove away from Charlotte Douglas Airport. He was still surprised that she'd agreed to come with him. Standing on her porch waiting for her to respond to his invitation, he'd seen the disbelief, then uncertainty dancing in her conflicted eyes. The *yes* that had floated out after several tense seconds came in a rush, leading him to believe she'd told herself to say it before she lost the nerve to.

Their drive to the airport had been quiet. Their flight had been quiet. Their trip now was quiet. Both acted as if at one point in life they hadn't been able to talk to each other for hours straight about anything. The weather. World issues. Clouds. Anything. They'd clearly lost that connection. But could a bond that ran soul deep completely fade? Even with space, time, and new love? Well, new love for her. He hadn't loved another woman since Macie. Sadly, he wasn't sure if he could. Trent ground his teeth. How freaking sad was that?

Trent wasn't sure how he felt right now. Wasn't sure how he was supposed to feel with the woman he'd loved and lost riding shotgun beside him. The fact that she'd broken his heart, shattered him to pieces, darkened many days for him should have been cause enough to hate her. He didn't.

"I could never hate you, Macie," he said, shattering the daunting silence. She eyed him in confusion. "Last night. You said I hated you." He shook his head. "I don't."

"Thank you for saying that."

He couldn't tell whether she believed him or not. But she had to know better, right? Heck, he'd asked her to come here with him. That wouldn't have happened if he hated her. Why did he even care what she thought or believed? He'd asked her here for one reason and one reason only. To satisfy an obligation. He would do just that, then kiss her goodbye. The kiss they'd shared in her bedroom filled his head and his lips tingled. Shake her hand goodbye, he corrected.

"I have to stop by the office. Do you mind or would you prefer I take you home first?" He baulked at his blunder. *Dammit.* "To my place, I mean."

His slip up didn't appear to faze Macie. She seemed just as poised now as she had sliding into the passenger seat of his rental back in Chicago. If she were uncomfortable being here with him, it didn't show. And if the ease she displayed around him was all a front, her acting skills were good as hell. He hoped his came across just as stellar.

"I would love to see your office," she said.

A smile that could outshine the sun lit her face. Something warm and tender swirled in his chest at the sight. Instantly, he rebuked the cozy sensation. Damn her for still having the ability to rouse something inside him.

Macie's jovial expression melted a bit. "Un…less you don't want me to go. If it would be awkward or something."

They'd ventured past awkward a long damn time ago. "I wouldn't have suggested it if that were the case."

"Yeah, I guess you're right." She turned away. "You said your place. I thought I'd be staying at a hotel."

Macie's words were hesitant. Almost as if she'd only asked out of formality. As if she hoped somewhere deep down that she'd be staying with him. Or maybe he was reading too much into it. But he didn't think so. Unfortunately, there was no other option. "There are several conventions happening. Every hotel my travel agent tried is booked to capacity. I have plenty of space at my place, but if you're more comfortable staying at a hotel, I can—"

"Your place is fine. It's not like we're strangers." A serious expression spread across her face. "Actually, I guess we are, huh? But not in an uncomfortable way. At least not for me."

Trent could tell that Macie wanted him to add *not for me either*. He didn't. Though, it would have been the truth. He was just as at ease with her now as he'd always been. It didn't make sense, but it did…if *that* made sense. Did uncomfortable even exist between two people who'd seen every inch of a each other's bodies, made unbridled love countless times, shared their darkest secrets and brightest hopes and dreams?

"We can get something to eat after we leave my office."

Her lips curled into a smile that barely touched her eyes, but she didn't respond. She simply turned away and plastered her gaze back out the window. Something was on her mind. Was she upset? Seriously, what exactly had she expected him to say? That it felt as if they hadn't spent a single day apart? That being here with her felt just like old times? That simply sitting this close to her had his system on full alert?

All of it was true, dammit. All of it. But he would not outwardly confess to any of it. No, he wouldn't allow her the satisfaction of knowing she still had some effect on him. He kneaded the stiffness at the crook of his neck, stress yanking his muscles tighter and tighter.

He hadn't been anxious before, but he sure as hell was now when realization of the situation he'd placed himself in came full circle. Inviting Macie here had been a huge mistake. Chemistry still lingered between them. That he couldn't deny.

His fingers tightened around the steering wheel at his stupidity. More than ever, he regretted not listening to that tiny voice in his head that had warned him not to climb back out of his car. Not to trudge back up her stairs. Not to ring the doorbell again. And definitely not to invite Macie to North Carolina.

He hadn't listened to any of it. Why did he have to be so damn stubborn at times?

Stupid, stupid, stupid.

What point was he trying to prove? That he wasn't still attracted to her? He was. To the point of losing himself a little each time their eyes connected. That she couldn't rouse a reaction in him? She could. That was apparent every single time they shared space.

Despite his regret, her presence here felt…on purpose and necessary. That scared him.

A short time later, they arrived at Thatcher Transport. Trent was surprised to see Brayden's night blue Porsche parked in front of the building.

"That's one sexy car," Macie said.

"It belongs to my business manager, Brayden Howard. She has a need for speed." The three speeding tickets she'd gotten that month alone were proof. Maybe it had been his imagination, but he swore he'd seen a mild dim in Macie's smile.

"She has great taste in vehicles," she said.

Inside, Macie took a seat in the lobby while he made his way to Brayden's office. He eyed the picture hung on the wall that highlighted the first truck he'd ever purchased. He'd acquired eight more since then. And soon, he'd add a dozen more to his fleet. Although his company was growing, and he was truly stoked about it, something felt…missing.

This leap of faith he'd taken with starting his own trucking company, this dream, had come at one hell of a steep price. Stopping, he tossed a glance in Macie's direction. *A hell of a steep price.*

When Trent entered Brayden's office, she was busy tapping away at the keyboard. "Hey," he said, visibly startling her.

She rested her hand over her heart. "*Shit.* You scared me."

"Sorry. What are you doing here?"

"I thought I'd come in and catch up on a few things that have fallen by the wayside as I worked on this deal." She waved her hand through the air. "Don't worry. Nothing important has gone unresolved."

He knew he didn't have to worry. Brayden always handled business.

Brayden removed a clipped stack of papers from one of the many piles on her desk and pushed it toward him. "Place your signature at each of the flags," she said.

Damn. Judging by the number of florescent-colored tags, he'd be there all day. Putting pen to paper, he said, "You know, you could have signed these. You sign my signature almost better than I do."

"That's forgery," she said.

As if she hadn't signed his name a million times before.

Her voice changed into something sappy. "Sounds like to me someone didn't want to leave Chicago."

He didn't bother looking up. "Whatever."

When Macie sneezed, Trent groaned. *Here we go.*

"Who was that?"

He could feel Brayden's gaze burning a hole through him. Without glancing up, he said, "Macie. And don't give me that look." The suspicious and accusatory one he was sure she was giving him. "It's innocent. I didn't want to renege on my obligation. You know I'm a man of high moral standards."

"Uh-huh." Brayden was quiet for a moment. "So, at what hotel did you say she's staying? I faintly recall your place only having one bed."

Trent laughed. "Could you let me concentrate, please?"

Brayden stood and rounded her desk.

Trent came to his full height. "Where are you going?"

"I want to meet her."

He blocked her path. "Why?"

"Any woman who can have a man still feigning after three years has some powerful juju. Maybe if I rub her belly some of it will come off on me. Plus, her meeting me is a surefire way to determine if she's still hooked on you, too. Though, I suspect she is. To trek from Chicago to North Carolina with you pretty much tells me she's not over you either."

"No one is feigning or hooked." But just out of curiosity—nothing more—he said, "And how in the world would you meeting her reveal anything? Other than the fact that you're nosy."

Brayden rolled her eyes heavenward. "Curious. And everyone—except you, obviously—knows that one thing that will make a man more appealing to a woman is a man who other women want." She held up her hand. "Don't get things twisted. I don't want you, but she doesn't know that."

Trent wasn't sure if he should have been offended or relieved.

Brayden continued. "Before she leaves, she's going to inquire about me, especially after I'm done. Now would a woman who didn't care about a man even waste her time doing so?"

Trent parted his lips to rebut, but Brayden continued.

"No, she wouldn't. You just finish signing the papers." She winked. "I've got this."

"This doesn't—" Before he could mount a full and proper protest, she snaked past him and out the door. "—sound like a good idea."

Seven

Macie held the Black Business Elite magazine in her hands, but it wasn't the business, love, and success article about billionaire Holton Channer that held her thoughts hostage. It was something else. Something that shouldn't have bothered her one single bit. Trent's business manager was a woman. A knot formed in her stomach. Not jealousy. Nope, not at all. Curiosity. Yeah, that was it. Curiosity.

No, it was definitely jealousy. Just a twinge. A bleep that shouldn't even exist at all. Why was she jealous? It wasn't like she'd come to North Carolina to win Trent back. Okay, maybe the idea had foolishly crossed her mind, but it was only a fantasy. An unattainable dream.

Stop this, Macie. Making an attempt to read the article again, her thoughts inadvertently drifted once more. How much time did they spend together? She bet a lot. *So, what if they did?* It wasn't any of her business. Her eyes lowered back to the page.

When asked what kept Mr. Channer grounded, he enthusiastically said his wife, whom he'd met when she held a temporary position as his executive assistant. Since there had been a strict non-fraternization policy in place at his company, he'd been forced to fire her before asking her out on a date. Macie laughed and continued to read.

The article went on to highlight their relationship, their family, and their twenty-year marriage. After finishing, she slapped the magazine closed, then placed it back on the steel and glass table in front of her. She sensed movement and glanced up to see an almond-toned, attractive woman moving toward her.

Was this Brayden?

The woman was gorgeous. Her hair was a shimmery cooper color that flowed in wavy locks down her back. She wore an expensive-looking, cinnamon-colored sweater paired with dark jeans tucked inside black, knee-high heeled boots. There was no masking what Macie felt now. Jealousy. Complex and pure.

"Hey," the woman said, jutting out her arm. "I'm Brayden Howard."

Macie stood. "Macie Shaw." She scrutinized the woman in front of her. From perfectly arched brows, hazel eyes, and tiny freckles dotting her cheeks and bridge of her nose, to her flawless skin, high cheek bones, and long model neck.

"Trent says you guys grew up together," Brayden said.

Brayden's voice snapped Macie back to reality. Was that all he'd told her? That they'd grown up together? "Um…yes, we did."

"That's awesome. Trent was one of the first people I met when I moved here from Richmond a couple of years ago. Then he wooed me away from my old job," Brayden said.

Wooed? How exactly had he done that? Macie had her ideas. Forcing a smile, she said, "He's a great guy." Why did she feel so salty toward Brayden? The woman hadn't done one single thing to her. Other than getting to spend countless hours with Trent.

Something dreamy flashed in Brayden's eyes as she

glanced toward the back of the building. "Yes, he is a great guy."

Brayden went on and on about Trent. How he'd always been there for her when she'd needed him. How good he was to his employees. How much they all loved him. She'd actually used the word love.

Two years, Macie thought. Trent and Brayden had worked closely together for two years. The Holton Channer article popped into her head, but she pushed it aside. She was being ridiculous. Trent never would have invited her to North Carolina if he and Brayden were involved. Casually or otherwise. He wasn't that type of guy. At least he hadn't been.

The why he'd described her to Brayden popped into her head. Someone he'd grown up with, not his ex-lover. He'd downgraded her to a mere friend he'd grown up with. "Is there—" Her words caught. "Is there a restroom I can use?"

"Are you okay?"

"Yes, I just need the restroom, please."

Brayden's expression morphed from bright and cheery to concerned. "Follow me."

Thankfully, Brayden didn't escort her into the sterile white room. Inside one of the stalls, Macie lowered the lid and sat. This trip was just full of surprises. Because of several conventions taking place, all the hotels in a thirty-mile radius were booked. The result, she'd be in close quarters with Trent, which hadn't seemed so bad until now.

What had she been thinking coming here? Clearly, she hadn't been thinking. At least, not with a straight head. Maybe she could lie and say Collette needed her back home. But why was she running? No, she would stay and show Trent that she'd gotten over him, too. Even if it was a lie.

After another minute or so, she got herself together and left her hideaway. She stopped halfway through the doorway when she spotted Brayden and Trent in the lobby engulfed in what appeared to be an intense conversation. Were they having a lover's quarrel?

As if sensing her watching them, Trent glanced in her direction. Something sparked between them. She hated how good and familiar it felt. And especially loathed how easily it sliced right through the layer of contempt that had been blooming inside her. Straightening her spine, she joined them.

"You ready?" Trent asked.

Macie nodded. "It was nice meeting you, Brayden." But was it really? Macie couldn't answer that.

"You, too," Brayden said.

The woman actually looked and sounded sincere. Oh, she was good.

"Call me with any updates," Trent said to Brayden, then escorted Macie out of the building.

"Everything okay with you and Brayden?" she asked as they walked toward Trent's truck. "You two seemed to be having a—" she caught herself before allowing lover's quarrel to slip out. "—heated discussion."

"We're fine."

We're fine. It certainly sounded like they were involved. "Good. I'm happy for you."

Trent eyed her with a slight crinkle in his brow, as if her response confused him in someway. Had she said it with attitude? Probably.

They arrived at Trent's place a short time after leaving his office. He explained to her how the converted brick building used to be an elementary school and how he'd fallen in love with his condo the moment he'd seen it. Once inside, she understood his draw to the place. Rustic brick walls, aged wood ceilings and exposed beams polished to a high shine. What she liked most about it was the open layout.

Although it was one level, the space was huge, spanning what seemed like a mile in either direction. The loft-style apartment surprised her because Trent had always talked about having a home with lots of land, an abundance of trees and a pond for fishing. She used to joke with him about being a country boy at heart. He'd always laughed, wrapped his arms around her and called her his country girl. She smiled a little at the memory, then forced the sentiment away. The memories of their old life together were too much to bear.

***

Trent flipped from one side to the other, entangling himself in the lone blanket covering him. *Dammit.* One thing for sure, had he ever considered the fact that one day Macie would be in his bed—and he'd be on the couch—he probably would have gotten around to converting his exercise room back into a spare bedroom. Or at least, would have invested in a sleeper sofa.

But how in the hell could he have *ever* imagined this?

Tossing his legs over the side of the sofa, he sat up. Leaning forward, he rested his elbows on his thighs, trying desperately not to glance in the direction of his bedroom. Unfortunately, the draw was too damn powerful. His attraction to her was too damn powerful. Her hold on him was too damn powerful. Or maybe he was just too damn weak.

Foolishly, he followed the sounds emitting from the room. Standing at the open door, he watched Macie sleep, but didn't enter the room. Tendrils of light from the full moon penetrated the blinds, washing the room in a warm glow. One of Macie's legs peeked out from under the covers. Longing thrashed inside him like an angry sea beat against the shore, as his eyes slowly trailed along her skin.

The many times those shapely legs had tightened around his waist—in the bed, against the wall, in the shower—made him smile. No woman had come close to drawing out the sexual beast in him the way Macie had been able to.

When Macie squirmed, it startled him. Snaking a hand between his legs, he adjusted the unwelcome erection. All he needed was for her to wake up and see him standing there with a hard-on. Hell, all he needed was for her to wake up to see him standing there period. But he couldn't walk away.

Macie's body writhed in a slow, sensual manner, and her moans grew deeper, longer. Was she dreaming? Gingerly entering the room, he stood a safe distance away. Yes, she was definitely dreaming. Something told him it wasn't G-rated.

Trent backed away to give her privacy, but when she said his name in almost a whisper, he froze. For a minute, he thought she was awake and had caught him there. She wasn't.

Was her dream about him? The idea did something to his ego…and his body. He swelled below the waist again. It was insane as hell, but he wanted Macie so bad right now that he felt lightheaded. How could anyone want one person this much? Especially one who'd cut him so deeply?

Macie went completely still and so quiet that he was afraid to move in fear of alerting her to his presence. A second later, she sucked in a deep, sharp breath that sounded similar to someone getting to breathe after having a plastic bag removed from over their head. Suddenly, she jolted forward and sat straight up in the bed.

He wasn't ashamed to admit that she'd scared the hell out of him. And when her eyes moved in his direction, and she released a blood-curdling scream, so did he. But in a gruff, manly sort of way, of course.

Macie fumbled with the lamp next to the bed. When the light came on, she squinted across at him. How in the hell would he explain this?

"*Trent*? What are you doing?"

Both Trent's brows shot up. "What am I doing?" he

echoed.

"Yes."

He massaged his jaw. "Oh. I was, um…I was in the kitchen. Drinking a glass of…w-water, when I heard sounds and stuff. I wanted to make sure everything was okay." Her expression gave nothing away, so he couldn't tell whether she believed him or not. "Is everything okay?"

"Yes. I guess I was dreaming."

"Ah. It must have been a really intense dream by the way you were moaning and squirming all over the place. I bet it was one of those dreams where someone was chasing you."

Her eyes darted away. "Maybe. I don't remember." Her gaze found him again. "All I remember is waking to see a shadowy figure standing there."

Trent pointed over his shoulder. "I should let you get back to sleep. Sorry for startling you." Something he seemed to keep doing. That morning in her hallway came to mind.

"It's okay. Thank you for checking on me."

Trent gave a single nod. Man, he was glad she didn't mention anything about his scream—er, gruff, manly release.

"What do you have planned for us this week?" she asked.

That was a good question. Instead of telling her he hadn't quite gotten that far, he said, "Tons of fun stuff."

Macie eyed him a moment. "You don't have anything planned, do you?"

"*Pssh.* What? Woman, I have tons planned. *Don't have anything planned.*" He massaged his jaw. "Oh, I've got stuff planned."

"Like what?" she asked.

"You'll just have to wait and see."

"How do you know I'll enjoy it?"

"Because I know you," he said. "*Used* to know you, I guess I should say. People change."

The excitement that had shone on Macie's face a moment earlier dimmed. "I haven't changed, Trent. Not that much. What I loved then, I still love now."

They stared at each other for a moment.

"I can't wait," she continued, snuggling back under the covers.

Strangely, neither could he.

Eight

After Trent had informed Macie earlier that morning that he needed to make an unexpected trip into the office to handle a personnel issue, she'd climbed back into his sinfully comfortable bed, wishing it were his warm arms cradling her instead of the pillow-top mattress. Unfortunately, sleep eluded her. There was too much on her mind. For starters, she couldn't stop wondering if there was something going on with him and Brayden.

Why did it even matter? She hadn't come to North Carolina to disrupt Trent's life. He'd built a wonderful life here. One that didn't accommodate her. She hugged a pillow to her chest and replayed the intensely tantalizing dream she'd had about him the night before and shivered. It wasn't the first time she'd dreamed about their lovemaking; it had, however, been the first time she'd orgasmed so hard it hurt.

Thinking about it made her moan softly. Trent's mouth, fingers, and manhood had gone places no man had ever been allowed to venture before. She'd liked. All of it. Evident by the release that had been so powerful it jolted her from her sleep.

And who had she found standing at the foot of the bed?

When she'd flicked on the light, the bewildered look on Trent's face was so amusing, she'd nearly laughed. She'd lied to him about not remembering the dream, but he'd lied to her, too. Though his explanation had been plausible—he'd been to the kitchen for water—it hadn't been the truth. At least not the whole of it. She knew this because she'd checked both the sink and dishwasher for a dirty glass and found nothing.

The way he'd casually mentioned her moaning and squirming pretty much confirmed he'd had an idea of the type of dream she'd been having. That fact should have mortified her, but it didn't.

Macie bit into her bottom lip. Staring at him in those gray sweatpants and white t-shirt that hugged his well-toned frame had sent her libido into overdrive. She'd wanted him. Right then. Right there. Desperately. Had wanted him to hold, touch, tease her. Do all the things he'd done to her in the dream. All of them. Especially make her come with the force of an earthquake. And the problem...she *still* wanted him.

Wanted his bare, hot flesh touching hers.

Wanted to experience their heartbeats dancing in tandem.

Wanted to feel the weight of his body as he moved in and out of her.

Wanted his hands moving all over her damp flesh.

Wanted to harmonize her moans with his groans as they climaxed together.

Wanted all of those things more than anything in the world.

Abandoning her lustful thoughts, she laughed at how Trent had screamed in response to hers. Obviously, she'd scared him just as much as he'd scared her. That deer-in-the-headlights expression on his face had made him look so adorable.

Another one of his expressions filtered into her head. The stumped look he'd displayed when she said, *What I loved then, I still love now*. Honestly, her words had baffled her a bit, too, once she'd considered the implication of them. There were countless ways to interpret the statement, but Trent appeared to have settled on just one. That she was saying she still loved him.

While it hadn't been her intent, maybe it had been her unconscious way of revealing a hidden truth. Even if she hadn't come right out and said it. But had she revealed too much? Would things get weird between them now? They had seemed normal when he'd left that morning. But Trent had always been great at hiding his feelings.

She groaned. Her life would have been so much simpler had she stayed in Chicago.

Her cellphone vibrated on the nightstand, startling her. Only one person would be calling her this early. "Good morning, Lette."

"So, have you two consummated your relationship, yet?"

Macie laughed. "There is no relationship to consummate."

"So, that's a not yet."

"I love your glass-half-full view of the world, but I'm only here because Trent needs to fulfill his obligation. That's it." Why did she think Collette would believe that lame excuse when she didn't even believe it?

"Remember who you're talking to, Mace. I'm your best friend. I damn near know you better than you know yourself. You're there because you want to be there. With Trent. You're where you've always wanted to be and always should have been. This is destiny at its best. This is fate giving you the second chance not many people get. Don't blow it by lying to yourself." Collette's tone grew compassionate. "You made a mistake, sweetie. One that cost you the love of your life. Don't make another one."

"I can't erase three years of heartache in just a few

days, Lette. And I'm not even sure Trent could forgive me."

"Something tells me he could. Otherwise, I don't think you would even be there with him. Just like you said yes for a reason, he invited you for a reason. And that reason has nothing to do with a damn bid."

***

The last place Trent wanted to be that Monday morning was in the office, which was crazy because, for the past several years, work had been his life. But today, cramming his morning with meetings, afternoon with conference calls and evening with reports, didn't seem all that thrilling. He knew why, and he didn't like it at all. Not one damn bit. Macie had only been in Charlotte a hot second and was already flipping his world upside down.

"What are you doing here? I thought you were out of the office today."

Trent glanced up from the incident report he'd been reading to see Brayden standing in the doorway. "So did I," he said. "Isn't it your job to handle shit like this," he said, waving the printout of one of his drivers' drive-time violation.

"I see you're still upset with me." she said, gingerly crossing the room.

Trent sighed heavily, pinching the bridge of his nose. His lack of sleep was making him grumpy. Softening his disposition, he said, "I was never upset with you, Brayden."

She eased down into the chair in front of his desk. "Oh, I beg to differ. Do you recall your reaction when I told you my plan might have worked a little too well?"

Remembering, he gave a single chuckle. Okay, maybe he hadn't taken it all that well when Brayden had told him she'd laid it on a little too thick and *sorta kinda*—her words—may have led Macie to believe something was going on between them, instead of her original plan to simply gage Macie's interest.

"Either way, it worked," Brayden said. "You know she still has feelings for you. Strong ones, obviously."

Trent didn't bother telling Brayden that Macie hadn't made a single inquiry about her. If she thought he and Brayden were involved, she clearly didn't care. Just as the thought faded, another filled its place.

What I loved then, I still love now.

Macie's words had felt weighted, as if they'd meant something far more than she was willing to own. Like she was somehow confessing that she still loved him. Did she? Trent immediately dropkicked the question from his head. Was he forgetting the hell Macie had put him through when she'd ended things? Why would he care anything about her feelings?

"What if I didn't want to know," he said, admittedly a little too harsh. *Shit.* He washed a hand over his head. "Sorry. I didn't mean to snap at you."

Brayden's expression turned sympathetic. "What's wrong, Trent?"

Her tone was so gentle and so kind that he toyed with revealing his turmoil. Ultimately, he decided against it, because he had no idea how to explain what was going on with him. "Nothing's wrong." His eyes fell back to the pages on his desk.

"You still love her, too. And you're driving yourself crazy over why and how you could still love the woman who broke your heart."

Trent's eyes rose, and his brows pressed together in confusion. *What the…?* How could Brayden possibly know this? Obviously, she recognized the question on his face.

"You could have easily flown back to Chicago to fulfill your bachelor obligation. Instead, you choose to bring Macie to North Carolina with you."

Trent gave an emotionless laugh. "So, that alone means I still love her?" He laughed again. "I just did what I always do. Follow through. Simple as that."

Brayden shook her head. "I can't tell if you really believe that or if you're trying to convince yourself to believe it."

Why in the hell was she giving him such a hard time?

"It was magical watching you two together, Trent. Standing there, I could feel your attraction to her. To each other. And boy, was it powerful."

For someone who rated relationships right up there with having a root canal without anesthesia, Brayden seemed awfully whimsical right now.

"The way you look at her. The way she looks at you…" Brayden's eyes twinkled. "It tells me your connection is still very much alive and strong. Even your body language was different when you were near her. Your posture was less rigid, less tense. Like being in her presence put you at ease. You seemed naturally relaxed. And the energy that bounced off you two… poetic. Yeah, you two are still in love."

"Loving Macie, *once*," he emphasized, "brought me a lot of pain that's not easily forgotten. I'm still wearing the scars. Those wounds have made me cautious."

"They've made you a coward."

Trent's brow shot up in disbelief. Had she really just called him a coward?

Brayden craned her neck. "Yes, I said it. In all the years I've known you, you've never run from a challenge. Are you sure you want to start now? When so much is at stake?" She stood, gave him a weary smile, then started for the door.

"For someone who bills herself as an opponent of love, you sure sound like an ally," he grumbled, because raw truth tended to make people grouchy.

Brayden stopped. A second or two passed before she turned to face him, a somber expression on her face. "I was Macie once. Unfortunately, I didn't have her courage when I needed it."

Trent's brows furrowed. "Her courage?"

"To seize her second chance." Brayden chuckled. "Do you really believe she followed you eight hundred miles just so you could satisfy an obligation?"

Obviously, she noticed the bemused look on his face.

Brayden huffed. "Of course, you did. Men." Moving away again, she stopped at the door. "Oh. Just for the record, I'm rooting for Macie."

***

It was a little after three when Trent returned home. Dead silence greeted him when he ambled through the door. His eyes swept the room. There was no sign of Macie. Had she gotten restless and gone site-seeing? A pinch of panic set in when he considered something else. Had she returned to Chicago?

Retrieving his cellphone from his pocket, he dialed her number. She answered on the third ring. The familiar background noise—specifically his neighbor's wind chime—led him to the window. Peering out, he spotted her in the courtyard. She wasn't alone.

While he didn't know the tall, brown-skinned man straddling the mountain bike, Trent had seen him around. Undeniable jealously, that he didn't even bother downplaying, seeped inside him. His grip tightened around his phone.

"Hello."

Macie's cheery voice danced over the line. Despite staring right at her, he said, "Hey. Where are you?"

"Outside. Are you here?"

"Yeah, I am."

Macie stood. "I'll be right up."

"Okay," he said, ending the call. He continued to observe her. When Macie tore a piece of paper from the leather-bound journal she held, scribbled something down and passed it to the guy, Trent ground his teeth hard enough to turn them to dust. Had she given him her number?

Obviously, Brayden had no idea what the hell she was talking about. *Second chance.* Macie didn't want a second chance. She was making a new love connection right there in his damn courtyard.

The voice of reason kicked in, reminding him that he had no claim to Macie. That she was free to do whatever—or whomever—she wanted. The idea of her being with another man knotted his stomach. Then it dawned on him. She had been with another man. Had nearly married him.

Trent moved to the kitchen and poured himself a glass of water, then propped himself against the counter and waited. A second later, he heard the just-in-case key he'd left for Macie slide into the lock. A beat after that, the door opened.

A warm smile touched Macie's glossy lips when she spotted him. "Hey."

"Hey," he said, taking another sip from his glass, then placing it on the counter.

Macie turned to place the thin black jacket she wore over the armrest of the chair. Trent took the opportunity to check out her backside in those form-fitting jeans. Heat charred the inside of his chest.

"It was so nice out I decided to journal outside. Is it usually this comfortable the first few days of April?"

Trent's eyes shot up. If Macie had any inclination he'd been ogling her behind, it didn't show on her face. He shook his head. "Um, no. No, it's not." She eyed him suspiciously, but didn't say anything. His attention lowered to the binder in her hand. "You're still doing that, huh?"

She placed the journal on the island. Trent would pay handsomely for access to what she'd written in there. Had she penned anything about him? Likely. Good, bad, or indifferent?

"It's my outlet. It keeps me sane."

He gave an understanding nod.

"I met one of your neighbors. Alec. He runs a web design firm. He's working up a quote to redesign my website. It's way overdue."

"That's…great," Trent said, fighting to keep his tone neutral.

"He seems really knowledgeable. Also, adventurous. He skydives, mountain climbs, scuba dives. He's—"

"*Wow.* He sounds like a real daredevil. You two should hang out." He added a lopsided smile to mask some of his cynicism. Even though he and Macie were only…only… Hell, he didn't know what they were, but drew the line at listening to her obvious captivation with the daredevil. A man had his limits.

"Funny you should say that. He invited me over to his place tonight. For drinks and such."

What the hell? Was she serious? She was going to his place for *drinks and such*? Oh, he could easily translate what the *such* meant. Something hot and unpleasant roared inside him, raising his temp several degrees. "You should go," he said dryly. "We can have dinner anytime." He fought to keep his disapproval in check, reminding himself that she was free to do whatever she liked.

"*We* should go," Macie said. "The invitation was for the both of us. I told him we had plans tonight, and he suggested we stop by on our way to dinner."

"Oh, I sincerely doubt the invitation was meant for the both of us. You go. I'd only be a third wheel."

Macie's head snapped gently, as if stunned by his comment. "Trent, you do know…"

Her words trailed, but he had an idea of what she had wanted to say.

He shrugged a shoulder. "Know what, Macie?"

She folded her arms across her chest in an almost defiant manner. "Nothing."

"That we're not together? Oh yeah, I definitely *know* that. Sadly, I don't think I'll ever forget the day you—" He stopped. *Dammit.* He'd just done the one thing he swore he wouldn't do during her stay. Dredge up the past. Lowering his head, he sighed. "Macie, I—"

She took a step toward him with fire dancing in her eyes, causing him to clam up.

"No. Don't attempt to backpedal. You have something to say, so say it. This conversation was inevitable, right? Now is as good a time as any to have it."

Trent washed a hand over his head. "I didn't invite you here for this," he said.

"Why exactly did you invite me here, Trent? So that I could see you've moved on? Well, I kind of figured you had. Brayden simply confirmed it."

He parted his lips to tell her there was nothing going on between him and Brayden, but changed course. "So, what if I have moved on, Macie? *You* moved on. You had a whole fiancé. And not that I need to justify myself to you, nothing has ever gone on between Brayden and me. Nothing."

Macie gave a condescending laugh. "Is that why you told her we were just *friends* who went way back, instead of lovers who were once so tight that we pierced each other's souls?"

Her voice cracked with emotion. By the way she straightened her shoulders, Trent knew she was trying to project a façade of strength that wasn't really there.

With an almost soothing tone, he said, "You were the one who walked away, Macie. Not me. You wanted to be free, so I let you go. Despite how much it hurt, I gave you what you wanted."

Macie shook her head. "No, you didn't, Trent. If you would have, we would still be together." Her gaze slid away, and she studied her feet.

In an exhausted tone, he said, "What did you want, Macie?" He shrugged. "What did you want?"

A beat of silence passed before her eyes met his again. "You, Trent. All I ever wanted was you. But you were off in another state, building your life in North Carolina, while back in Chicago, mine was falling completely apart."

Falling completely apart? Macie's words jarred him. Had she gone through something and kept it from him? His anger morphed to concern, then fear. "What does that mean?"

Macie rested a hand over her collarbone, her fingers seemingly searching for something that wasn't there. Her lips parted, but closed. Finally, she said, "It doesn't matter now, Trent. That was the past." She retrieved her journal. "I'm going to lie down for a while."

With his options limited to simply accepting what she said, he nodded.

When Macie disappeared down the hall, he chastised himself for allowing his emotions to take over. Moving to the sofa, he stretched out and closed his eyes. He needed a second or two to quiet all the noise in his head.

It was close to two hours later when Trent opened his eyes again, awakened by a thud. He checked his watch. *5:15*. Good. He hadn't slept through their 7:00 dinner reservation. Sitting forward, he rolled his stiff neck. Sofa sleeping was definitely not for him.

Figuring Macie was more approachable now, he decided to pick up where they'd left off. Despite her unwillingness to elaborate earlier, he had to know what she'd meant by that life completely falling apart statement. Had she struggled financially? Emotionally? What?

Coming to his feet, he stretched his tight muscles, then made his way down the hall. He froze when he saw Macie, his brain going blank for a second or two. The sight of her in the off-one-shoulder black dress snatched his breath away. The curve-hugging fabric fell just below the knee and a small split ran a little ways up her thigh. Why was she getting dressed for dinner so early? A bitter answer came to him. *The daredevil.* He didn't even know the man, but hated him.

Could he really allow her to go alone? Anything could

happen. The daredevil could drug her, then take advantage of her in the subdued state. Could force her to do unsavory things. Hold her captive. Torture her.

Okay, now he was just being ridiculous. The truth was, he didn't want her alone with him, especially not looking so damn sexy. His reasons were more selfish than precautionary ones.

Macie glanced up to see him standing there, but she didn't say anything.

"Um, hey," he said. "You look…great."

"Thank you." She sat on the edge of the bed. "I'll be back before we need to leave for dinner," she said, sliding into a pair of strappy black heels.

Trent slid his hands into his pockets. "I can go with you, if you still want."

She glanced up. A delicate smile curled her lips but faded as if she hadn't wanted him to see her delight.

"Are you sure?" she asked. "I don't want you to feel like a third wheel or anything."

He wasn't sure about a damn thing: why she was going to hang out with his neighbor, why he cared, why it felt like betrayal when she hadn't been his for a long time. Despite all of that, he nodded. "Can you give me a couple of minutes to take a shower and dress?"

"Yes."

One thing for sure, this was going to be an interesting evening. He could feel it.

Nine

Their argument was unfinished. It was what Macie told herself as she eased down onto the bed and waited for Trent to dress. Maybe they would have finished had she not said too much. Why had she let the words slip out? *While my life was falling completely apart*. She knew Trent, and he wouldn't stop prying until she told him what he wanted to know. Maybe he deserved to know, especially since it played a huge part in why she'd ended things with him.

"Knock, knock."

When she glanced up to see Trent standing in the doorway, wearing nothing but a white towel fastened low on his hips, her mouth went dry as sawdust. Shamelessly, her gaze traveled over his damp chest, then trailed along a mid-section far more defined than she remembered. A line of curly dark hairs disappeared beneath the towel. Her core tingled knowing what gloriousness lingered there—and how good he was at using it.

Her heart rate kicked up a notch and breathing grew unsteady thinking about their past intimacies. One thing Trent had always been good—make it great—at was pleasing her. Her body didn't shy away from reminding her of that now. All her sensitive areas buzzed with awareness of him. She prayed her beading nipples stayed concealed by the fabric of her bra. However, she held little hope the lacy material would mask her arousal.

"I need to grab something from my closet," he said.

Trent's words tore Macie from her stupor. "O…okay." She pulled her reluctant-to-leave eyes away. Making a desperate attempt to not stare at him as he moved to the closet, she failed miserably. His sculpted back flexed with every move he made. Her fingertips ached to trace the contours of him.

Would making love to him now feel the same? Better? If it were any better than it once had been, she wasn't sure she could handle such a conflict to her system. While her ex had been okay in the bedroom, he'd never taken her to the sexual peaks Trent had. Justen had been familiar enough with her body, but had never taken the initiative to truly get to know it thoroughly. Again, not like Trent had. Trent had always known what, when, and how. Like he was a homing device her body sent signals to.

She snapped out of her daze when Trent turned to face her. He lifted a black button-down shirt as if to say, got it. When he left the room, she breathed a little easier. But her body still reacted as if he stood in front of her. *Traitor.*

A short time later they walked in deafening silence to Alec's place, located two levels up from Trent's. She could feel the tension wafting off of Trent in thick sheets. If she had to guess, this was the last place he wanted to be. So why hadn't he stayed home? A tiny smile curled her lips. He hadn't wanted her to be alone with Alec. Though he hadn't said as much, she was sure of it.

Inwardly, she chuckled. She hadn't lied to Trent about Alec, just hadn't told him everything. In her defense, she'd attempted to share more information with him, but he'd seemed far more determined to believe she would come all the way to North Carolina with him just to cozy up with his neighbor, than to listen.

Men. Always jumping to conclusions.

"Our reservation is at seven," he said.

"I know, Trent. You've reminded me three times."

Before he could counter, the door opened. Laughter and chatter poured out.

"Macie," Alec said with excitement, pulling her into a hug. "I'm so glad you made it."

Macie swore she'd heard Trent grumble. "I wouldn't have missed it for the world," she said. Despite barely knowing Alec, they'd clicked like old friends.

Alec released her and turned to Trent. "And you must be Trent."

Trent nodded, his expression a mix between cordial and anxious.

Alec extended his hand. "It's nice to finally meet you, neighbor."

"Same here," Trent said.

"Come in, come in." Alec stepped aside and allowed them to enter.

Alec's place was not as spacious as Trent's but was enough to accommodate the thirty or so people in attendance comfortably. Macie couldn't resist tossing a glance in Trent's direction. Just as expected, confusion was etched deep in his expression. And when Alec introduced them to his husband, Kashmel, you could have knocked Trent over with a feather.

The second Alec and Kashmel left them to their own devices, Trent turned to her, a plethora of questions burning in his narrowed eyes.

"Had you taken a moment to listen to me, I would have told you we were attending an anniversary gathering. You chose to think so little of me that you convinced yourself that I would hook up with your neighbor. Shame on you," she said.

"That's not fair, Macie."

"Is it not true?" she challenged.

Trent's jaw clenched tight, and his eyes burrowed into her. The stern look on his face told her that he wasn't exactly pleased with her at the moment. However, his silence confirmed her accusation.

"I was jealous," he said.

The admission stunned her.

"But I didn't have a right to be. You're no longer mine."

With that he walked off.

Macie allowed him his space for a while before eventually joining him and the group he'd been chatting with. He acknowledged her with a weary smile when she stood so close to him, their arms touched. Electricity speared her soul.

"I was jealous, too," she whispered to him. "When I thought you and Brayden had something going on."

Trent opened his mouth to speak, but Kashmel's high-pitched voice drew both their attentions.

Kashmel waved Alec over to him, then took his hand. "We just want to thank everyone for coming out tonight to celebrate this amazing night with us. Old friends, new friends." Kashmel tipped his glass toward Macie and Trent, then eyed Alec affectionately. "I don't have the words to express how much I love this man."

The room filled with sounds of affection.

"Alec, you are my heartbeat, my best friend, my shelter in the storm. If it wasn't for you, I wouldn't be standing here today. You brought me back from a dark place. You breathed life back into me."

Macie rested her hand over her heart, unshed tears burning her eyes.

"You've seen me through good times and bad, through laughter and tears. You've loved me at my worst. You've loved me at my best. My life began and will end with you. There's no one on this earth I'd want to spend my forever with. Happy anniversary, Bear."

Applause rang out when they kissed. Macie ran a hand

across her cheek. She could feel the love radiating between Alec and Kashmel. It reminded her of what she and Trent once shared. A swarm of emotions rushed her all at once. "Excuse me," she said to Trent before taking off in the direction she hoped to find the bathroom.

Inside the sage-colored room, Macie took a deep, calming breath, then blew it out slowly. Listening to Kashmel heightened her feelings for Trent and reminded her of all she'd lost. Tears welled in her eyes, and she dabbed them away. "Pull it together, girl," she mumbled to herself. Scrutinizing her appearance in the mirror a second or two, she left the room. Outside the door, she collided with Trent.

Macie drew in a sharp breath, unsure if it were a result of her shock or the surge that traveled through her when Trent's arm wrapped around her waist. "You startled me."

"Are you okay?" he asked.

"I'm fine. Just got a little emotional. I'm such a softy sometimes." She managed a wobbly smile.

He stared at her as if trying to ascertain whether or not to believe the claim she'd just made. The lines crawling across his forehead smoothed, his shoulders relaxed, and he let his arm fall. "One of your most endearing qualities."

"You kissed me," she said. "The night you drove me home from the auction." Unsure why she'd chosen this moment to blurt the words, she waited for his response. The timing couldn't have been worse, but hey, did matters of the heart ever have the ideal moment?

The lines returned to Trent's forehead. But these didn't resemble lines of confusion like the ones before; they looked more like ones of torture.

***

Trent had known kissing Macie that night had been a bad idea. But he hadn't considered his actions would come back to bite him in the ass. How in the hell had she even remembered their lips touching? Cleary, she hadn't been as out of it as it had appeared.

Standing here now, staring into her delicate eyes, made him feel like some kind of pervert who'd taken advantage of her. That hadn't been the case. He'd simply been unable to resist. Perhaps he'd been a fool to believe that there was a way such intense fervor could have stayed hidden away in her head.

"I did. I'm sorry. It was bad judgment. I never should have—"

"Don't apologize," she said.

Don't apologize? Macie's tender expression suggested she'd liked the kiss. Did she recall anything beyond their tongues intertwining?

Had she felt what he'd felt?

As light as air, carefree and absolutely content.

Had she experienced what he'd experienced?

His entire body awakening from her touch, their connection.

Had she wanted what he'd wanted?

To make unbridled love to her all night long.

No, she couldn't have.

If so, they'd be having a much different conversation than they were having now. Unsure what to say next, he glanced at his watch. "We should probably get going."

The brief expression on her face translated to *is that all you have to say.*

Instead of protesting, she nodded and led the way to the front.

They said their goodbyes to Alec and Kashmel, wished them a lifetime of love and happiness, then made their way to his truck. When Macie slid into the passenger seat, her dress rose, flashing Trent a bit of skin. All he could consider was placing slow, gentle kisses to the inside of her thighs. The stir inside his boxers demanded he banish the thought.

With each passing second, he wanted Macie more and

more. But he'd never used his dick recklessly and wouldn't start now. And that's exactly what sleeping with Macie would be…reckless. Especially when he knew for certain that a night with her would corrupt his entire system. And he'd gone through too much hell purging her from it. But fragments of her still remained, which made him more susceptible to falling for her again.

Rounding the vehicle, Trent blew a hard breath. He didn't want to admit that he was in peril, but he was. If his lips met Macie's again, he wouldn't be able to pull away so easily. That made her dangerous. He also didn't want to want her as much as he did. She was becoming the most intense craving he'd ever had in his life.

He couldn't afford to fall into the trappings of love again. He'd clawed his way out once and didn't plan to place himself in the position to have to do so ever again. *Ignore this soul-nourishing attraction*, he told a body seemingly far more eager to welcome than resist her.

Ten

The second they stepped inside Harpie Johnson's, Macie's eyes swept the interior of the popular Creole restaurant. The décor made it feel as if she were dining at an establishment in Louisiana's French Quarter. The sights and sounds were reminiscent of the trip she and Trent had taken there years ago. She studied the large alligator head draped in colorful beads. Its open mouth served as a mint holder. The piece definitely could be described as unique.

She waited as Trent gave his name to the hostess. A moment later, they were led to their table—marble topped with four wooden chairs upholstered in clover green fabric. The single candles that flickered in the center of each table gave the room a romantic ambience. She tried not to feed too much into the intimate atmosphere.

"This place is lovely," she said as Trent slid out her chair.

"It's one of my favorite spots. The food is amazing."

So, he'd been here before. This wasn't the kind of place one dined at alone. Had he come for a business meeting? With friends? On a date? The latter possibility bothered her a bit too much. Like Trent had said, she'd had a whole fiancé, so why was she troubled by his dating.

"I pick up take out here so often they know my order by heart."

"Crab-stuffed poppers, spicy crab pasta with extra crab and beignets. Heavy on the sugar."

Macie eyed the dark-skinned, older gentleman dressed in all black floating toward their table. He had an immaculately-trimmed beard and sideburns both peppered with gray, close-cropped salt and pepper hair and sported a burgundy fedora hat tipped to one side.

Trent stood and gave the man a firm shake.

Mr. Smooth Flowing clapped Trent on the shoulder. "Trent Thatcher. Always good to see you, my man."

When Trent introduced him as *The* Harpie Johnson, Macie offered her hand. Harpie Johnson's hands were calloused, like he wasn't a stranger to hard work. It reminded her of her father's. A man who'd worked tirelessly to provide for his family. And he'd done a fantastic job of it. Macie swallowed the swell of emotion rising in her chest.

"Enchanté, mademoiselle," Harpie said, then kissed the back of her hand rather than shake it.

"Delighted, as well, monsieur."

Harpie's brow lifted. "Understands and speaks French. I'm impressed."

"I only speak a little," Macie said.

After a few more minutes of small talk, Harpie thanked them for coming and moved away.

"You know the owner, huh?" Macie said. It didn't surprise her. Trent had the kind of personality that drew people to him, and the man never met a stranger.

Trent shrugged one shoulder. "Impressed?"

"Are you trying to impress me?"

"I imagine you didn't spend five-thousand dollars to be underwhelmed with your trip to North Carolina."

Macie gawked at him several seconds. "I'm impressed,"

she finally said.

Trent gave her a lopsided smile. Probably because he knew she really wasn't. He, of all people, knew it took a lot to impress her. She'd never been easily dazzled. A quality she'd inherited from her mother.

She refused to dwell on any memories of her mother for fear of bursting into tears right here at the table. Though both her parents passed years ago, the pain still lingered. Why was she so emotional tonight?

Their waitress arrived to take their drink orders. She recommended the Big Easy Blitz—a champagne, Chambord, Grand Marnier, lime and cranberry mix and the French Quarter Sangria—white or red wine, cherry brandy and plenty of fresh fruit. Macie chose to stick with tea. She'd gotten her fill of alcohol for the remainder of the year. Trent chose the same.

When the young woman strolled off, Macie pinned Trent with a steady gaze. "I'm proud of you. You've done great for yourself. Made all your dreams come true."

"Not all of them," he said.

She waited for him to elaborate. When he didn't, she continued. "Well, you know what they say. It's never too late to go after your dreams."

Trent pushed his brows together as if he were confused. "I wonder why people say that. It's never too late."

"Probably because it's true. Do you not believe that?"

"No," he said without hesitation. "Everything eventually comes to an end."

His answer surprised her. At one point, Trent had been the most optimistic person she'd ever known. "Dreams don't have an expiration date. As long as you have a heartbeat you can pursue them."

"*Mmm*," was his only response before lowering his gaze to his menu.

The waitress returned with their drinks and took their food orders. Jambalaya for Macie. Chicken and sausage gumbo for Trent—because he'd felt like trying something different, he'd said.

Macie took a sip from her glass. "Whoa. That's sweet. But I like it," she said.

Trent chuckled. "Sorry. I should have warned you. Tea's a little sweeter here than it is back in Chicago. But it grows on you." Trent studied her.

"What?"

"A dry cleaners? It probably shouldn't surprise me. You were the only person I knew who actually found solace in ironing."

"When I returned to Chicago, I needed a change. I wanted to do something different. I asked God for a sign." She laughed. "Boy, did I get one. Literally."

"Well, that piqued my curiosity. What happened?"

"Collette and I were leaving Sweet Cakes Bakery." She paused when Trent gave her a look. "What?" Though she already knew. It could be said that she had a slight obsession with the cupcakes at the popular establishment. Trent had been sent there countless times for an assortment of tasty goodies.

He grinned. "Nothing."

She rolled her eyes playfully. "*Anyway*. Walking down Hammond Drive, a *sign* fell right in front of us. Men were removing signage for the cleaners that once occupied the space. The place was for sale. Several weeks later, I owned Precision Dry Cleaning."

Trent nodded slowly as if mulling over her words. "I'm proud of you, too," he said. "You've done great for yourself as well. What about your dreams? Have they all come true?"

Macie eyed him for a long moment before answering. "I'm still working on them."

For the next hour or so, they ate, chatted, laughed. Laughed some more. And some more. It felt like old times. After all that had transpired between them, after all the time that had passed, Trent could still amuse her and was still so easy to talk to. She'd missed their conversations, had truly missed him, but until this moment, she hadn't realized just how much.

After stuffing herself with the best jambalaya she'd ever put in her mouth, she miraculously found room for bananas foster. Instead of ordering two of the savory desserts, she and Trent shared one massive serving. Of course, he ate the majority, revealing that he still had a ravenous sweet tooth.

Leaving the restaurant, Macie breathed in the crisp, chilly air as they strolled toward Trent's vehicle. The aromas from the restaurant filled her nose, reminding her of the delicious meal she'd just eaten. "I enjoyed the food and conversation," she said.

"So did I," Trent said.

Inside the vehicle, he started the engine, placed his hand on the shifter but didn't put the truck into gear. Instead, he angled toward her.

"What did you mean when you said your life was falling apart?" he asked.

She knew this would resurface but hadn't expected it to so soon. Sliding her gaze away from him and training it straight ahead, she sighed.

"You can tell me none of my business, but—"

"I was attacked, Trent," she said, cutting him off.

Her gaze found his again. He sported a mix of shock and confusion. Understandable. Once the initial stun visibly wore off, his face contorted, morphed, relaxed, then changed to stone, void of any expression at all. The look filled her with something, but she couldn't explain what.

"Y—?" His words caught. He looked away briefly, cleared his throat, then continued, "You were attacked?"

His tone was steady, calm, but the rapid rise and fall of his chest alerted her to his distress. As tempted as she was to shutdown, leave the ugly past where she'd buried it, she didn't. "The night…The night you were supposed to fly home. Back to Chicago," she said for unnecessary clarity.

"The trip you cancelled. Again," she added, instantly regretting how accusatory she sounded. She studied her twiddling fingers. "I was so upset with you. It felt as if I was becoming less and less of a priority in your life. That night…" She eyed him again, "I didn't want to be alone."

Trent slouched in his chair. Maybe he thought she was going to say she sought the comforts of another man. She would have never disrespected him that way.

"Collette and I went to The Renaissance Lounge for a few hours. I came home, took a shower and was preparing for bed when I heard a noise downstairs."

When Trent looked away, she couldn't help but wonder if he was recalling the horrific trauma in his own past, when his father had been murdered during a home invasion and mother assaulted and left for dead. The memories it would have conjured for him was a minor reason why she'd kept it from him when it happened. The main was because she'd selfishly blamed him. If he'd only been there like he was supposed to have been…

Witnessing how this was affecting Trent, Macie wanted to stop talking, but in a strange way, telling him felt right, like a boulder was being lifted off her. Unfortunately, the weight was clearly being transferred to him. That hadn't been her intent.

"I dialed 911 but told myself I was just being paranoid, so I hung up. I went downstairs to make sure everything was *locked up tight*." It was what Trent used to say to her every night right before they ended their usually hour-long phone conversation. "*Yes, sir*," she would respond. If her symbolism registered with him, it didn't show in his expression, which was still set in stone. "Anyway, I noticed my backdoor was cracked."

Trent curled his fingers into tight fists in his lap, and he didn't look at her when he spoke. "Macie…" His words dried up. When he started again, his voice was strained, shaky. "Did he—"

"No. No," she repeated, thankful she hadn't been

violated in the same way his mother had. "Apparently, my call to 911 had gone through. And when they'd dialed back and hadn't gotten an answer, a unit had been dispatched to my location. I guess the glow of their headlights startled him. That and—" She stopped.

Trent eyed her. "That and what?"

She debated giving him an answer. "I cried out for you."

A puff of air escaped from Trent as if he'd been punched in the stomach with an iron fist. His head fell back against the rest as if he was too weak to control his neck muscles. Closing his eyes, he released a sound that was a blend of a grunt and a growl. He didn't speak again for a long time, and she didn't rush him, simply allowed him to process what she'd just told him.

Finally, his head rose. "Who was it?"

Macie wouldn't have recognized his voice had she not been sitting right beside him and witnessing his lips move. "I don't know. There had been this asshole who'd gotten overly aggressive when I rejected him at The Renaissance. The police seemed to have believe he may have followed me home. But honestly, it could have been anyone."

Trent struck the steering wheel. "Why didn't you tell me, Macie? Why didn't you call me?"

"I did," she said, her tone equally as forceful as his.

A confused expression spread across his face. Then, as if a lightbulb went off in his head, he said, "The following morning. When you ended things. You blamed me."

"Yes, I blamed you. I blamed you for not being there. I blamed you for not protecting me. I blamed you for everything. But none of it was your fault. I was just too frazzled, too filled with anger, too hurt and disappointed at the time to see that. And when I finally realized the mistake I'd made, it was too late. The damage had already been done."

"Who knew this happened to you?"

Macie was sure he was attempting to ascertain whether

or not Mama Peaches knew and hadn't told him. She didn't, because while Mama Peaches had never broken her trust, Macie knew this situation would have been the one exception. "No one. No one but Collette."

Trent dragged an open hand down his face. "*Jesus.*"

Trent finally drove away from the restaurant. Things between them were quiet for a long while as he drove back to his place. Clearly, he was as lost in his thought as she was in hers.

"I waited for you, Macie," Trent said, breaking the silence. "I waited for you to come back to me. I didn't stop waiting until I learned you were engaged. At that point, I knew it was really over. You belonged to someone else and was about to become his wife. It hurt like hell, but I finally let you go."

Was he trying to tell her something?

***

Trent needed a damn drink.

What Macie had told him after they'd left Harpie Johnson's had not only pained him to his soul, but had also conjured up some ugly memories. If the police hadn't come, would Macie have ended up like his father—taken from them too soon by some worthless piece of human waste? Or like his mother—so traumatized by the event that she'd slowly detached from reality and had drank and medicated herself into an early grave? Losing her at nineteen had been hard, but he'd had Macie.

Macie. His eyes slid toward the bedroom.

Retrieving a bottle from the cabinet, he poured himself a shot of cognac and swallowed it in one gulp. *I cried out for you.* Those words would haunt him until his dying day. He refilled his glass and down it with the same haste as the first.

A part of him understood why Macie had kept this from him. A part of him didn't. She'd sheltered and alienated him at the same damn time. And as if learning what had happened to her hadn't hurt enough, she'd blamed him.

Feeling defeated, he pressed both palms against the chilly countertop, leaned into them, and lowered his head. Maybe she'd been justified in blaming him. If he hadn't cancelled his trip, she never would have gone out and given some bastard an opportunity to follow her home. She would have been safe in his arms instead.

He pulled open his anything drawer—the one drawer in his kitchen where *anything* could be found—and removed the black velvet box stashed in the back. Popping the top, he stared down at the reason he'd been forced to cancel his trip that day. A three-carat princess cut engagement ring blinged back at him.

He'd wanted the element of surprise. He'd had it all planned out: surprise her by showing up the following the day, take her to lunch, then visit the Cultural Center and propose to her in the exact spot he'd first proclaimed his love for her.

It hadn't worked out that way.

He'd been the one who'd gotten a surprise, receiving Macie's call just as he'd arrived at the airport to fly to Chicago. Listening to her end their once-in-a-lifetime type of love, he hadn't put up a fight, hadn't questioned, hadn't said much, because he couldn't. What he had done once the call had ended was shatter into a thousand jagged pieces.

Trent shook the devastating memory away, along with the pain that still lingered for losing his one true love. Losing Macie had been his biggest and most regrettable failure. Spending forever with her had been the one dream that hadn't come true.

"Trent?"

Startled by Macie's gentle voice, he closed the box and hurried it back into the drawer. When he turned to face her, the tempting-as-hell black dress had been replaced with a royal blue and white pajama set. Her beaded nipples pressed against the fabric of the spaghetti-strap top. He tried to ignore them.

"I can leave tomorrow, if that's what you want," she said in a soft tone.

The statement drew his complete attention. While he didn't want her to leave, he also didn't want her to feel obligated to stay. "What do you want, Macie?"

Her eyes left him and settled on the floor as if she were unsure about what she wanted or knew but was trying to figure out how to tell him. Trent's eyes never left her. Several seconds ticked by before she brought her gaze back to him.

"You," she said.

Eleven

Even without the dazed look on his face, Macie knew she'd taken Trent completely by surprise. But he wasn't the only stunned one. One minute the words had been bouncing around in her head, the next they were escaping past her lips.

Trent stared at her as if he was trying to figure out if he'd actually heard what he'd thought he'd heard. His confusion was warranted. She'd never been impulsive. Yet, here she was, issuing him one hell of a risky challenge. If he accepted it, great. If not, she would feel like one helluva fool.

Well, she'd come this far. No use in backing down now. When another wave of confidence washed over her, she moved so close to Trent that her breasts pressed into his chest. Her nipples hardened even more, causing a painful ache only the warm suckle of his soft lips could relieve. Cradling his face between her trembling hands, she brought his mouth to hers and brushed his lips with a light kiss. The resulting spark ignited her entire body.

Staring into his eyes, she said, "Should I walk away?"

Trent's lips parted, closed, parted again, closed again.

When they parted a third time, he said, "Yes," in a tone barely audible. It could have been the way his eyes were fixed on her mouth or his solid erection pressing into her stomach or the rugged pacing of his breathing that led her to believe he didn't truly want her to go anywhere.

Testing her theory, she pressed her lips to his again, this time allowing them to linger. She waited for him to respond. Finally, with measured movement, Trent's mouth opened and allowed her eager tongue to invade the warm space.

The kiss started off noncommittal but quickly grew in fervor. One of Trent's arms wrapped around her waist, holding her firmly in place. The taste of fine cognac flavored the inside of his mouth. Their tongues danced in perfect harmony, then battled one another for dominance. Trent was still the best kisser she'd ever known.

"I want you, Trent. Even if it's only for tonight," she managed to say against their joined mouths.

Without warning, he scooped her into his arms and carried her to his bedroom. With so many tantalizing sensations flowing through her, she barely registered him placing her on her feet. She wasted no time undressing him. She wanted—no, needed—to see him in all his naked glory. With unsteady hands, she managed to unbutton his shirt and push it over his shoulders, causing it to fall into a black puddle at their feet.

As if awed by the landscape of his chest, her fingers gingerly explored his smooth, heated flesh. Touching him seemed to give her strength. That had never happened with her ex. Flattening her hands, she glided them over his pecs. Her eyes rose to his when his heart drummed against her palm. Each beat empowered her more and more.

Her hands fell to his belt, but they shook so horribly she couldn't unfasten the buckle.

"Let me," he said.

Trent removed the leather accessory with ease, then unbutton his pants but didn't push them off his hips.

Instead, he grabbed the hem of her shirt and lifted the fabric over her head, then guided her to the bed. The second she was atop the mattress, he lowered his head and took one achy nipple into his mouth. Instantly, she experienced relief and pleasure that she acknowledged with a deep moan.

He licked, flicked, and suckled, then moved to her opposite breast, giving it an equal amount of attention. His hand snaked down her torso, past her waistband and inside her panties She squirmed with anticipation. His thumb pressed against her swollen clit and circled it slowly. When he curved two fingers inside her wetness, she cried out.

Trent kissed his way down her body. Removing her bottoms and panties, he spread her legs and peppered warm kisses to the inside of one thigh, then the other. When his warm lips found her core, she sucked in a sharp breath. Within seconds, heat blossomed in her stomach and coursed all through her body. She didn't want this delicious torture to end, but was powerless against the orgasm building inside her. Several more swipes of Trent's tongue sent her careening over the edge.

Her back arched off the bed and she wailed in ecstasy as the intense release lifted her to a peak she hadn't reached in a while. Blood whooshed in her ears as the pulsing between her legs seemed to go on forever. Still buzzing, she eased down, and Trent licked and nipped his way back up her body.

After lavishing her with another magnificent kiss, he shucked his pants, reached into his nightstand and pulled out a gold-wrapped condom, angled to one side, and sheathed himself. When he entered her, she wrapped her legs around him and rode each one of his powerful thrusts.

It wasn't long before the clutch of another orgasm tightened around her. "*Trent*," she screamed. She wasn't the only one reaching their breaking point. Trent's movements slowed, became clumsy. A few strokes later, they came together in a chorus of grunts, moans and cries.

Trent collapsed to his side, then rolled onto his back, bringing Macie with him like a lover he couldn't risk escaping his bed. In silence, they snuggled against one another. While insinuating no commitment, this felt like the start of something. Of what, Macie had no idea.

She refused to allow the uncertainty to ruin the beautiful moment they'd just shared. Tonight, she would pretend Trent was all hers. Tomorrow, she'd face whatever consequences that would stem from their actions.

***

Trent should have been drained, but he wasn't. He and Macie had made love all Tuesday night and into Wednesday morning. They'd made love Wednesday afternoon and into that evening. They'd made love into the wee hours of Thursday morning. The only thing that had kept them from spending all day in bed was the fact that they had plans.

Keeping them had been a challenge. Especially when all Trent wanted to do was make love to Macie. After all of their lovemaking, he still hadn't gotten enough of her. The woman was like a drug he just couldn't stop. Clearly, he wouldn't be satisfied until he'd overdosed on her.

Trent had no idea how they actually made it to the Wilson Air Center by their scheduled time, but somehow, they had and with ten minutes to spare. After a flight safety briefing, they were off on their helicopter tour of uptown Charlotte and Lake Norman.

"This is amazing," Macie said into the headset she wore, a huge smile curling her lips.

"I thought you'd like it," Trent said, attempting to display a level of happiness he didn't truly feel.

When she set her gaze back out the window, the glow on his face dimmed. The anguish he felt was a result of his own doing. He'd known the second he'd welcomed Macie into his bed, he would regret not having stronger willpower. He'd broken his own rule, but it had been so worth it. At least for right now. Would he feel the same way when she boarded her plane back to Chicago?

Thus far, the only thing he regretted was the fact that she would be leaving in two days, leaving him with nothing but memories. At least they'd be good ones. But would that be enough? He couldn't believe he was even posing these questions. Had he forgotten she'd ripped his heart out of his chest? Left him picking up pieces of himself?

His cellphone vibrated in his pocket, jolting him from his thoughts. He read the text message from Brayden. She was letting him know that all paperwork had been filed and the sell was officially a done deal. The news should have overjoyed him. Strangely, it didn't.

"Everything okay?" Macie asked, concern spread across her lovely face.

He nodded, then stashed the device back in his pocket. "Perfect."

After their helicopter tour, Trent whisked Macie away to their second destination. She'd seen the Queen City by air, now she needed to see it by land, via a guided Segway tour. It was only a short drive to South Tryon Street, which left them plenty of time to check-in and sign the waivers that would absolve the company of any liability if they broke something, or something broke them.

The only other time Trent had been on a Segway was when he'd taken all of his employees on an hour-long fun ride a year or so back. All had appeared to enjoy it, and so had he. He hoped Macie would, too. At first, she'd been skeptical about riding *something with only two wheels*, as she'd put it, but had warmed to the idea after a gentle nudging.

The two-hour tour carried them to Levine Avenue of the Arts, Panthers Stadium, the Historic 4th Ward, and several other locations, including some of uptown's best restaurants where they sampled either appetizers, main dishes, or desserts from each location.

"Oh, my God, that was so much fun," Macie said as

they walked back to his truck. "I can't believe I was afraid. I think I'm in love with Segway riding now."

"Do you want to come back tonight for the haunted Segway tour?"

She answered him with an eye roll.

"I'll take that as a no."

"Actually, that was a hell no. You, of all people, should know I don't do haunted anything."

He did; he just wanted to see if it still rang true. She truly hadn't changed that much.

"I'm having a phenomenal time, Trent. I didn't realize Charlotte had so much to offer. No wonder you love it here so much. I guess there's no getting you back to Chicago, huh?"

Trent wasn't sure if it was a question or a comment. And since he didn't want to respond with *his life was here now*, he considered it to be the latter, then changed the subject. "Are you hungry?"

Macie stopped and shifted toward him. "Are you kidding me? We stopped at like six restaurants on the tour." Her brows crinkled. "Are you still hungry?"

He shrugged. "I mean, if someone strolled past offering doughnuts, I wouldn't turn them down."

Macie jostled him playfully. "You and that ferocious appetite."

Yep. But the only thing he truly had a taste for right now was her. He would starve when she left. But he'd survived a Macie famine before; he would again. At least, he hoped.

Twelve

Macie and Trent arrived at Charlotte Douglas with plenty of time to spare before her flight back to Chicago. Trent pulled into one of the spaces in the parking garage and killed the engine. Obviously, he intended to walk her inside. Macie wasn't sure if that was such a good idea. While the circumstances were different this time, she still knew walking away from him again would be just as hard as it had been the first time.

When she'd agreed to come to North Carolina with him, she'd held a fantasy of working her way back into his heart. Sadly, that hadn't happened. With each passing day, she'd foolishly hoped Trent would give her some sign, a hint that he wanted to try again. That hadn't happened either. Surprisingly, she was content with it. Just seeing him so happy was enough for her. If anyone deserve to be, it was him.

She'd cherished their time together but knew she would have to let him go. For good this time, if she ever wanted to move forward with her own life. Despite the fun-filled days and beautiful nights they'd spent together, their season had obviously passed.

"You don't have to walk me in," she said.

Trent flashed her one of those gorgeous smiles, and her stomach fluttered. Damn him for still having such an effect on her system.

"What kind of host would I be?"

"One who didn't have to walk a thousand miles back to his vehicle."

They shared a laughed.

Trent rolled Macie's luggage as far as he could inside the terminal, stopping when he couldn't go any further. "Well, I guess this is it."

Standing toe-to-toe with him, Macie stared into his eyes. "Thank you, Trent."

His brow furrowed. "For what?"

"For giving me exactly what I wanted and needed. Over and over again." She smirked. "But mostly for reminding me what it feels like to smile again." She tamped down her emotions. "You're a good man, Trent Thatcher. You're going to make someone an extremely lucky woman." She'd be lying if she said she wasn't upset that the someone wouldn't be her.

"Thank you," he said, his expression not as gleeful as it had been moments earlier.

She kissed his stubbled cheek. "Goodbye, Trent Thatcher." Something told her this would be the last time they crossed paths. Sure, she could suggest they be buddies, but there was no way they could be friends; she loved him too much. "Be good to yourself."

Trent rested his hands on either side of her neck. He kissed her back, but not on the cheek. To her surprise, he captured her mouth in the hungriest, greediest, rawest kiss she'd ever experienced in her life. Her legs went weak. Whispers and giggles sounded from those who passed them by, but that didn't appear to faze him.

When he pulled away, her lips ached from the delicious assault on her mouth.

"Goodbye, Macie Shaw," he said. "Keep following

your dreams."

Trent's lips parted as if he wanted to say more. She wanted him to say more. Ask her to stay. Confess that he still loved her. Anything. He would have to make the first move. When he didn't, she turned but didn't move away. Facing him again, she said, "Because of you."

Confusion lit his expression. "What does that mean?"

"You asked me once why I called off the wedding. The truth is, I called it off because he wasn't you." With that, she turned and walked away. With each step, she hoped Trent would say or do something to stop her. She didn't give up hope until the plane was in the air.

***

Trent had known he would miss Macie, but damn, he had no idea he would miss her this much. The smell of her sweet, fruity fragrance still lingered inside his bedroom and permeated his master bath. The scent brought back some tantalizing memories.

At the airport almost a week ago, he'd been convinced that not telling Macie he wanted her to stay had been the right decision; he wasn't so sure now. What did he expect would happen had he told her? That she would uproot her entire life to join him in North Carolina? Abandon her business? Abandon her friends? Abandon her life? To be with him?

Because he wasn't you. The words had played on rotation in Trent's head since Macie had told him the true reason why she'd called off the wedding. Why in the hell had he not stopped her from getting on the plane right then?

Pouring coffee into his insulated mug, Trent headed out the front door. When he arrived at Thatcher Trucking, his vehicle was the only one in the lot. But at five in the morning, it usually was. Typically, he was the first in and the last out most days.

At 6:15, Brayden strolled into his office, plopped down

in the chair across from his desk and donned an oddly dreamy look on her face.

"What's wrong with you?" he asked.

She swooned. "I had the most *amazing* evening. *Amazing*," she said. "I've never been on a date so perfect."

Date? Brayden didn't date. Trent pushed his keyboard aside and gave her his full attention. "Do tell," he said.

"Well, you know I loathe dating, especially blind-dating, but I said hey, why not? I don't want to be old and lonely, wishing I'd taken that one chance that could have led me to a lifetime of happiness."

The way Brayden looked at him, she'd clearly been trying to send him an offhand message. He ignored it.

She continued, "It's like this man was created just for me. Educated, a great job, no kids—which means no child support. No wife. No ex-wives—which means no alimony." Her expression dimmed a bit. "He is a widower, though."

"And?"

"What if he's vowed to never marry again to honor his dead wife or something like that?" she said.

Trent barked a laugh. "Aren't you the one who said, and I quote, 'Marriage is for suckers'?"

Brayden buried her face in her hands. Coming up, she said, "I know, I know. But there's just something about this one. I can feel it."

Trent had to admit he'd never seen Brayden so enthralled over a man. "Well, if you're happy, I'm happy."

"But are you really?" she said. "You've been a little mopey lately. I think you miss Macie. I think you know you two should be together. Have you at least called her?"

He chuckled. "No, and I don't plan to. I'm happy. Macie's happy. Everyone is happy."

Brayden shook her head and stood. "Old and lonely," she said before leaving his office. "Old and lonely," she called out again. "Call her, Trent. Call her."

Trent eyed his desk phone.

***

While Macie hadn't lied to Collette about her happiness for Trent and all he'd accomplished in Charlotte, she had told a humdinger of a tale when her friend had asked if she missed him. She'd said no. But truth was, her heart hadn't stopped aching since she'd boarded her flight home a week and a half ago. The only communication she'd had with Trent since she'd returned home had been a generic text he'd sent making sure she'd made it safely.

Pride wouldn't allow her to admit how much she longed for Trent, not even to her best friend. She'd accepted karma's revenge, a life without the man she loved. Something tightened in her chest at the reality.

Why hadn't he given her a sign, just a tiny hint that he'd wanted her in his life? Probably because he hadn't wanted her disrupting his cozy existence. He'd given no indication her absence would even haunt him one iota. Foolishly, that angered her because her nights and days were spent fantasizing about him, while his were more likely spent wining and dining someone else.

"Did you hear what I said, Macie?" Collette asked from the opposite end of the telephone line.

Not a word. "I'm sorry. What did you say?"

"I had a dream."

"About what?"

"Not what, who. You and Trent. Standing at the altar, gazing lovingly into each other's eyes. The moment was so real that I could smell the roses and calla lilies in my maid-of-honor bouquet. And when you recited your vows to one another, I cried. When I woke this morning, my pillow was wet."

Macie swallowed hard. "That sounds like one heck of a dream."

"It was so vivid that it felt more like a premonition. Fate is not done with the two of you, hun. I'm as sure of that as I am my own name."

Hearing the conviction in her friend's voice brought water to Macie's eyes. *Always the optimist.* When she blinked, several tears trickled down her face. Swiping her cheek with the back of her hand, she drew in a deep breath to wrangle some semblance of control. "Sorry, Lette. I think fate has called it quits on Trent and me. I'm okay with it." Because she had no other choice but to be. "I still—" She stopped when her cell phone beeped, indicating an incoming call on her other line. Eyeing the screen, she gasped. "It's…*Trent*," she said more to herself than to Collette.

"Answer it," Collette said, excitement radiating through the phone.

"O-okay," Macie said. "I'll call you later."

"You better. It'll give me the opportunity to say I told you so."

Macie wished she had Collette's confidence about how things would turn out. Running her fingers though her hair as if Trent could see her though the phone, she said, "Hello?" in a low, causal tone.

"I never should have let you get on that plane," Trent said in lieu of a customary greeting.

His words dumbfounded her. "Um…" She wasn't exactly sure how to respond. Finally, she shuttered out a shaky "W-why?" It seemed like the most sensible question at the moment.

"Because I didn't want you leave. I just didn't know how to say that, how to get out of my own way to say it."

Macie ambled across the kitchen and eased down into one of the chairs around the small nook table. "Oh."

"Macie…" His words dried up. Continuing after a few moments, he said, "I'm absolutely miserable without you. And I have been for three years."

"I'm—" Macie jolted when a lawnmower started nearby. *Jesus.* Peeping through the blinds, she saw neighbor pushing the mower between the two houses.

"Let me finish before you say anything, Macie. Please."

"Okay," she said.

"I didn't think I could ever hurt as much as I did when my mother passed. I was wrong. When my mother died, I had you to lean on, to help me through. When you ended things, I had no one, Macie. I was devastated. My hurt turned to sadness, then to despair, then to anger. I was angry as hell at you."

She wanted to tell him how sorry she was, but the words wouldn't make their way passed the painful lump in her throat.

"I wanted to be over you, *needed* to be over you, because holding on to you was killing me. And I thought I was over you. Then I walked into the dry cleaners and saw you there. Something filled my heart, replenished my soul. I tried to ignore it. And then you came to Charlotte. Our time together revealed something."

"What did it reveal?" she asked. Trent went silent as if considering whether or not to answer her. Anticipation of his response made her jittery. "Trent?" she prompted. For a moment she thought he'd disconnected, but she still heard the roar of the lawnmower. Maybe he— *Wait. Lawnmower?* Why did she hear the lawnmower over the phone? Her heartbeat kicked up a notch as she came to her feet. "Trent, where are you?" Her tone was low, cautious.

"Exactly where I want to be."

Macie moved to the front of the house, rested her hand on the knob, took a deep breath, then pulled the door open. She gasped at the sight of him standing there.

"It showed me that I can't live life fully without you," he said, ending the call.

"You're…you're here," she said. Her heart banged so ferociously in her chest, she was surprised Trent couldn't hear her rib cage rattling.

Trent moved toward her. Slowly. Seductively. Purposefully. "Forgive me, Macie."

"For—" She stopped when she realized the phone was still pressed to her ear. Lowering it, she continued, "For what?"

"For not consistently showing you how important you were to me. For only considering my wants and not yours. For living a life where you weren't right there by my side." Trent cradled her face between his hands. "Everything I did back then, Macie, I did for us. But I should have taken the time to ask you what *you* wanted for us. I was selfish, thoughtless, and it cost me far more than I ever could gain. It cost me you, and that was too high a price to pay."

"You're not the only one at—"

Trent silenced her with a kiss that buckled her knees. When he ended the delicious connection, their chests rose and fell in sync. He rested his forehead against hers, and she took the opportunity to steal a peck.

Capturing her hand, he placed it over his beating heart. "I love you, Macie Renee Shaw. I've always loved you, and I know I always will."

Tears streamed down her face. "I love you, Trent Caswell Thatcher. I've *always* loved you, and I know I always will."

Trent smoothed the pad of his thumb across Macie's cheek. "Are you willing to place one more bid?"

Macie reeled back and pushed her brows together in confusion. "One more bid? What kind of bid?"

Trent eyed her sternly. "A bid on forever. Baby, I promise to love, honor, cherish, respect, and satisfy your ever need." He gave her a wicked grin. "*Every* need."

She arched a brow. "It sounds like you're proposing some tantalizing nights."

Trent took a step back, reached into his jacket pocket and pulled out a box. "Actually, I'm proposing far more than that."

Macie gasped, dropping her cell phone. When Trent went down on one knee, she stumbled backwards. "Trent…" Her words faded when he revealed the large diamond inside the box. It took her breath away. It was the most gorgeous ring she'd ever seen. And it sparkled as if a thousand lights shone on it.

"Macie, I've spent too much time foolishly blaming you. All I want to do now…" He paused a moment. "All I want to do now is spend the rest of my life loving you."

For a brief moment, Macie thought she was dreaming. Was this really happening? Everything in her heart and soul told her it was.

"I know you probably think I'm crazy right now, but that's okay. I am. I'm crazy over you. Woman, I love you with every cell in my body. And I need you. I need you," he repeated. "So, Macie Renee Shaw, will you marry me?"

"Yes. Yes. Yes." Macie lowered to her knees in front of Trent and cradled his face. "I would say yes a million times, because I would—" She choked on emotion. "Because I would bid a million forevers on you."

Epilogue

Macie waltzed into the kitchen with a smile big enough to eclipse the sun. Two things contributed to her happiness. The first was the sight of her husband standing at the sink, sipping coffee, wearing nothing but a pair of fitted boxers. God, that man's body could stop a riot at a wig shop.

Quietly, she stood admiring him. Every single day, she fell more and more in love with this man. If anyone would have told her that she'd be married to Trent one day, she would have called them a liar. Actually, someone had told her. Collette. She recalled the dream her best friend had had and smiled. Maybe it had been a premonition after all.

Though they'd made their home in Charlotte, Macie and Trent had chosen to say their vows on a warm July evening in the gardens of the Southlake Cultural Center, surrounded by family and close friends. They were approaching their one-year anniversary.

Creeping up behind him, she wrapped her arms around his waist and rested her head against his warm back, kissing him gently on the shoulder. "Good morning, Mr. Thatcher."

Trent set his cup down and rotated in her arms. "Good morning, *Mrs. Thatcher*." He closed his arms around her. "I really love the sound of that."

"And I really love you," she said.

He lifted a Pantone and pointed to several colors. "I've narrowed it down to these three for the spare bedroom. What do you think?"

The fact that he wanted her input made Macie smile. Taking the Pantone, she tilted her head to one side and stared at the variation of browns. She shrugged one shoulder. "They're okay, but I think a pastel pink or baby blue would be perfect."

Trent barked a laugh. "Baby, those are nursery colors."

This brought her to the second thing that contributed to her happiness. "I know." She bit the corner of her lip, waiting for Trent to catch on.

"So, why would—" He stopped, awareness spreading across his face.

Macie removed the plastic stick she'd stashed inside her waistband and showed him the positive pregnancy test. "You're going to be a daddy."

Trent cradled her face. "We're pregnant?"

Tears filled Macie's eyes at the sight of them filling Trent's. She nodded. "Yes."

He lowered to his knees, lifted her shirt and peppered her stomach with kisses. "Hey there, lil man—"

"Or lil girl," Macie said.

He glanced up at her and shook his head. "It's a boy. I can feel it." He refocused on her midsection. "But it doesn't matter what you are, little one, because I already love you. You have a pretty cool dad, but your mommy…she's totally freaking awesome. We are two of the luckiest people on earth. I can't wait to meet you." Trent rose to his full height and wiped Macie's tears away as she wiped his. His voice cracked when he said, "You keep giving me life, woman." He kissed her gently on the lips, then pulled away, resting his forehead against hers.

"Forever, bumblebee."

Macie latched her mouth to his and kissed him in a way she hoped conveyed just how much she loved him. Ending the kiss, she placed her hand over his heart. "Forever."

Seven months later, they welcomed eight-pound, six-ounce Trenton Caswell Thatcher II into the world.

ABOUT THE AUTHOR

By day, Joy Avery works as a customer service assistant. By night, the North Carolina native travels to imaginary worlds—creating characters whose romantic journeys invariably end happily ever after.

Since she was a young girl growing up in Garner, Joy knew she wanted to write. Stumbling onto romance novels, she discovered her passion for love stories. Instantly, she knew these were the type stories she wanted to pen.

Real characters. Real journeys. Real good love is what you'll find in a Joy Avery romance.

Joy is married with one child. When not writing, she enjoys reading, cake decorating, pretending to expertly play the piano, driving her husband insane, and playing with her fur baby.

Joy is a member of Romance Writers of America and Heart of Carolina Romance Writers.

Other Books by Joy Avery:

Indigo Falls

His Until Sunrise (Book 1)
His Ultimate Desire (Book 2)

The Lassiter Sisters

Never (Book 1)
Maybe (Book 2)
Always (Book 3)

The Cardinal House (Kimani Romance)

Soaring on Love (The Cardinal House, Book 1)
Campaign for His Heart (The Cardinal House, Book 2)

Kimani Romance

In the Market for Love

Standalone

Smoke in the Citi
Cupid's Error
One Delight Night
A Gentleman's Agreement
The Night Before Christian
Another Man's Treasure

Other Books in the Distinguished Gentlemen series:

- *Lover's Bid*, A.C. Arthur
- *An Outlandish Bid*, EJ Brock
- *The Bid Catcher*, Anita Davis
- *Switched at Bid*, Nicole Falls
- *The Renegade Bid*, Kelsey Green
- *The Contingency Bid*, Sherelle Green
- *The Birthday Bid*, Suzette D. Harrison
- *The Reluctant Bid*, Sheryl Lister
- *Losing the Bid*, Suzette Riddick
- *The Rival Bid*, Reese Ryan
- *Invitation to Bid*, Angela Seals
- *The Closing Bid*, Elle Wright
- *The Alpha Bid*, Ty Young

Where you can find Joy:

WWW.JOYAVERY.COM
FACEBOOK.COM/AUTHORJOYAVERY
TWITTER.COM/AUTHORJOYAVERY
PINTEREST.COM/AUTHORJOYAVERY
AUTHORJOYAVERY@GMAIL.COM

Visit Joy's website to sign up for the Wings of Love Newsletter

Be sure to follow me on:
AMAZON
BOOKBUB

53003623R00076

Made in the USA
Columbia, SC
14 March 2019